THE MOON AND THE WIND

BY

A. P. CARROLL

M. EVANS

Lanham • New York • Boulder • Toronto • Plymouth, UK

M. Evans
An imprint of The Rowman & Littlefield Publishing Group, Inc.
4501 Forbes Boulevard, Suite 200, Lanham, Maryland 20706
http://www.rlpgtrade.com

10 Thornbury Road, Plymouth PL6 7PP, United Kingdom

Distributed by National Book Network

Library of Congress Cataloging-in-Publication Data Available

ISBN 13: 978-1-59077-483-0 (pbk: alk. paper)

THE MOON AND THE WIND

I

"BUT I don't *like* fish!" shouted Gloria Newcombe, the top-ranking star of IMPORTANT PICTURES, INC.

"Look, Gloria. *Look,* Gloria! Will you just listen for a minute? For just one little *minute?*"

"But I *have* been listening! I've been listening to you for days, and what do I hear? *Fish!* That's what I hear. Honestly, Moe, if I didn't know you better than your own grandmother I'd think you were in some kind of a plot to drive me completely crazy! Look at me, Moe. You know what I'm like. You know how I am about fish."

"Do I know about it! Can I ever remember anything else? And has it driven me nuts? You know the answer."

Moe Wurtzberg, the well-known Hollywood agent, threw himself into his chair with such violence that the springs squeaked. Unlike many agents, who are men with eyes of glass and breasts of granite, Moe possessed a heart so sensitive that it throbbed to all the emotions of his stars like an Aeolian harp exposed to the winds. When they stormed, he stormed; when they cleared up and began to smile, a ruddy light illuminated Moe's honest, rocky features like dawn over the coast of Maine. But the trouble with Moe was (and all his friends told him so. from the best to the bitterest) that he reacted just as sympathetically to the changing moods of his stars' producers, directors, husbands, script-writers and publicity men. His tender breast was perpetually buffeted with the waves of anger, jealousy, fury, pride, hope, despair and rapture which swept from location to office, from office to cutting room, from cutting room to boudoir—and he swayed and resounded and frothed to all of them. Thus you could always tell when Moe had been having a session with anybody of importance in Hollywood, and if you knew the people in pictures you could even guess just who the personage was, for Moe would have absorbed his mood so completely that until he met somebody else he was more like the personage than the original was himself. You may think this made Moe a bad agent. It didn't; it made him one of the best on the continent. He was the most faithful sounding board in Hollywood, and anybody who wanted to know anything about anybody had only to come to him. It was extremely valuable that Moe was sensitive and impressionable, for the stars and the producers tried out their tantrums upon him, and, observing the result, could then proceed to check, revise, and improve them to the very best advantage of everyone except Moe himself. For if Moe was good for them, they were certainly hell on Moe, and it was always a question whether his arteries would hold out much longer.

Now it happened that Gloria Newcombe was a sweet and warm-hearted girl, and she could not bear to inflict needless pain upon anyone. Indeed, Gloria was very much like those gentle people who wander into tailors' shops through no fault of their own, and are measured for twenty costumes on the spot, when all they came in for was a package of needles and a spool of thread, number 70.

The trouble was, though, she really couldn't bear the very idea of fish in any form—and if ever she was so unfortunate as to eat even the minutest portion of one of these dull, dank creatures, she immediately got sick, had a fever, and came out in spots.

So when the executives of IMPORTANT PIC-TURES, INC., observing the huge success of *Furious Fins, a Romance of the Grand Banks,* and seeking a new vehicle for their most valuable star, set their minds and their teeth upon a saga of the salmon industry in Alaska, you can well imagine that Gloria was hurt and despondent, not to say desperate.

Add to this that her contract had expired and she refused to sign a new one, that her feeble-handed husband was shaking her down for more and better money, and that she had never wanted the husband or the contract in the first place, and you have something of a problem for Moe Wurtzberg's nervous system. (The husband was feeble-handed in the sense that he could never resist a dollar. Fifty dollars made his hand trem-ble; a hundred made it shake; but the trouble was, it always shook them into his pockets.)

And why hadn't Gloria wanted the contract in the first place? Chiefly because she was an opera star, both in talent and in temperament, and she enjoyed opening her mouth wide and making a fine, rich noise a lot better than she did murmuring amorous nothings into the ears of a good-looking moron who couldn't sing as well as she could, but who had box-office appeal and an elegant profile. As for *her* profile, she didn't like it nearly as well as her full-face, and she preferred to have people out in front who were listening to her voice and not looking at her nose. And now all this about fish! Really, it was too much.

It was too much for Moe Wurtzberg, anyway.

"Now come, Gloria. After all I've done for you, you might at least do this one little thing for me. You don't have to eat any fish. You don't have to sleep with them or talk to them. All you have to do is lend yourself to the glamor of this really fine, primitive theme while clucks like me do all the dirty work."

"Dirty work is right," said Gloria. "Dirty work is exactly what I'd call it."

Moe's big jaw quivered, and he got up and strode to the window. With his back to her, he stared out into the speckled sunshine of her garden. All this damn sunlight! He was sick of it. If only there were some nice Newark fog, some good old Newark snow, instead of this perpetual flash and glitter of yellow and blue and green, this lushness, this profusion! He'd be hanged if he didn't chuck the whole thing and go back to good old Chadwick Avenue.

As he stood there brooding, he heard a light step and felt a soft hand on his cheek. "Darling, I didn't mean it. You know I'm grateful to you. You know I'd do almost anything for you. I think you're an angel."

"Now look here, Gloria," he cried, turning round. "Don't you do that. Don't you go making me sorry for you. You know I can't resist it."

"Angel!" Gloria cooed. "Come sit down over here and let me get you something cool."

"Now listen, Gloria, this isn't fair. You know how I am." His large face was breaking into smiles.

"I knew you'd listen to reason, darling," she said sweetly, in her very best voice, which was so good that it cost five-fifty to hear it at the Metropolitan if you were lucky enough to get a ticket, and if your name wasn't Swope or Vanderbilt or something like that you probably weren't. "Come, baby—come with mama."

He ambled along beside her, waving his huge hands. "I haven't shifted my position an inch!" he shouted. And with a tremendous sigh, he sat down and closed his eyes. "Make mine a Daiqueri. Weak."

"I'll make it so weak you'll love it," she murmured. "Here. Rest your head on this pillow."

He sighed again. Good old Hollywood! There was something about it, just the same. Maybe he'd stay on awhile.

When Gloria's butler brought his drink he sipped it ruminatively. Good old Gloria! She had feelings. She wasn't like those cannibals in the producing offices of IMPORTANT PICTURES, INC., who cared for nothing but money and stayed awake nights devising new ways to drive him crazy. Fish, indeed!

II

"THE salmon are running!" said Mr. J. Coddington Rapaport (né Jake Rapaport of the Washington Heights Rapaports), head of production and Executive Vice-President of IMPORTANT PICTURES, INC. "It'll be terrific! Tremendous! Get that crook Wurtzberg on the phone."

"Yes, Mr. Rapaport," said Mr. John G. Humphries, Special Administrative Assistant to the Executive Vice-President. And he rushed into his office and looked his secretary sternly in the eye. "Get me Wurtzberg!" he commanded.

"Get Wurtzberg!" said the secretary into the streamlined talking box upon her desk.

"Yes, Miss Lexington," said the talking box, with a throaty gurgle and a bzzz-bzzzz.

Moe Wurtzberg was having a heavy dream about white elephants and whales, in which it seemed that the largest and stubbornest representatives of each tribe had got together to elect an arbitrator of their mutual difficulties, and the choice had fallen unanimously upon Moe. They were now exerting considerable pressure upon him to accept the appointment and get to work; so much pressure, indeed, that it seemed a question whether Moe would survive it unless a few of them climbed off of him.

If it hadn't been for the bell, he would have been a goner.

"Oh!" said Moe. "Ohhhhh!" And he struggled weakly out of a sea of pillows and books which seemed to have snowed him under through no fault of his own. Shoving the six volumes of Gibbon's *Decline and Fall* and the complete works of Victor Hugo from their resting place on his chest, Moe reached for the phone beside his bed.

"Hell and oh!" he said.

"Mr. Wurtzberg, Mr. Wurtzberg, IMPORTANT PICTURES have been calling the office again! What will I do?" It was his secretary, a Miss Hooper, speaking.

"Didn't I tell you what to tell them?" said Moe sternly.

"Yes, Mr. Wurtzberg, but they just said get Wurtzberg, and I couldn't think of any answer."

"Oh! You couldn't think of any answer."

"Well, not exactly, Mr. Wurtzberg. What answer is there?"

"I don't know! Why are you asking me?"

"But Mr. Wurtzberg, what will I tell them?"

Moe groaned.

"What was that, Mr. Wurtzberg?"

"Stop calling me Mr. Wurtzberg! All I ever hear these days is Mr. Wurtzberg, Mr. Wurtzberg, Mr. Wurtzberg! I tell you, I'm going nuts."

"What is it, Mr. Wurtzberg?" Miss Hooper could be sweet that way.

"Nuts, I said!" Moe groaned. "That's what I'm going.

You keep away from Daiqueris, Miss Hooper, because they creep up on you and before you know it people will be calling *you* Mr. Wurtzberg."

"Very well, Mr. Hoo—Mr. Wurtzberg. But what will I tell IMPORTANT?"

"Tell 'em I'm right here! Been waiting to hear from them all day! I'll tell them where they get off at. Get me IMPORTANT right away. Hop to it, Miss Hooper."

He sighed and lay down again. The world was definitely not a kind place for a man of quiet, calm tastes and an extremely weak stomach, who only wanted to be let alone.

The bell jangled again. To Moe it sounded very much out of tune. He gritted his big teeth and picked up the phone. "Hello," he said. "Is that you, J. C.?"

"Yeah, yeah, that's me," said the voice of Mr. J. Coddington Rapaport, Executive Vice-President of IMPORTANT PICTURES, INC. "How are you, old boy? Feeling good?"

"I'm fine, J. C." Miss Hooper, listening in, waited for him to growl, but Moe melted to a palsie-walsie gurgle. "How are you, kid?"

"Great, Moe, just great."

"Say, I'm delighted to hear that, J. C. What's on your mind?"

"Nothing much. Things pretty stale around here."

"That so? I heard it too, around town, but I didn't pay much attention. Well, that's certainly tough, J. C."

Moe's brain was functioning on all twelve cylinders now.

"Yeah. I'll tell you a secret, between you and the next feller, and if you should spill this to simply anybody I'm telling you you get no consideration from me from this day forth. Get that?"

"You can count on me, J. C. Would I let you down?"

"Nah, nah, you wouldn't—otherwise why am I telling you? Well, listen, Moe. I was just talking to Fancher. (Little Abe Fancher, the president, starting with a poverty-stricken "quickie" company, had really put IMPORTANT in the big money.) Y' know what I think we need over on this lot is a little new blood. See what I'm getting at?"

"I've been thinking that for some time myself, J. C., but I didn't want to say anything, because—"

"Yeah, yeah, yeah. So listen, between you and me I'm looking for a new star who can give it everything —looks, voice, singing, dancing, the unspoiled type, one of these simple daughters of nature or maybe from a small town at least—you know what I mean?"

This conversation began to make sense to Moe. He certainly did know what J. C. meant.

"Sure, J. C., I see what you mean," he purred. "Somebody to step into the lead in that salmon epic, or whatever it was, since Gloria Newcombe ain't interested."

"Nah, nah, it's something else a little more intriguing I'm thinking of. She wouldn't be interested. Forget about Gloria. Well, give me a ring some time next week if you happen to run across a type. I'll do what's fair for the right layout. You know me. But forget Newcombe."

"Sure, sure, J. C. Well, I'll keep an eye out off and on. Good-bye."

There was a mirror over Moe's bed and as he hung up he caught his eye staring back at him with an expression of bored unconcern that made him furious. "They're desperate!" he cried. "I can smell this herring a mile." He glared into the mirror and dialed Gloria's number.

"Hello?" came her voice, like some exquisite, far-off bell.

"Hello, kid. How are you?"

"Who is this? Is that you, Moe?"

"Yeah, yeah, of course it's me. You feeling good?"

"Moe! You've been talking to old oyster-face. Haven't you?"

"Who, me? Should I waste my time talking to him? Listen, kid, I want to tell you something. Promise me you won't spill this to a living soul. I found out indirectly that things over at IMPORTANT are simply red-hot. They're wild, kid, wild! We've got them to a point now where they'll be willing to sign you at double your first contract and with any support you want. They're howling for you!"

"Moe."

"What? What *is* the matter?"

"Moe. I want to ask you one thing. Just one little thing. It isn't important—understand? Just a whim of mine, only a whim. You know how we girls are about our whims, though."

Moe put one of his hands to his head. It was beginning to feel as if there were an ache coming.

"Why of course, Gloria. Anything at all. You know me."

"Just one thing. No fish!"

"Now listen, Gloria, I've tried, and I've tried, and I've contrived, and I've done everything a reasonable mortal man could, and now I want to tell you that I've just come to the point where— Hello! Hello! Operator! Hello!"

But the phone only buzzed mockingly in his ear, like a sea-shell with a bad cold.

III

WITH a delicious shiver Gloria relaxed in the water
and let the little ruffling waves lap over her gently. It
was cool, cool, and wonderfully good. No worries here,
nothing at all but the delight of contact with water and
air, of springing muscles and supple strength. She
heaved a long sigh, swept her arms over her head, and
plunged straight down till she touched the bottom of
the pool. M'm! Nice down here. Then she shot up to
the surface, slapped the water into a shower of sparkling drops, and laughed with joy as they came tinkling
down on her head.

A pair of sad, red-rimmed eyes watched her from the
rim of the pool. Where Gloria moved, they moved;
what Gloria did, they reflected within themselves like
a pair of faithful mirrors. "Ah me!" said the eyes, or
would have said if eyes were capable of saying anything.
"Alas!"

"This woman," said the eyes, "is young, happy,
healthy, and the slickest thing in a bathing suit we have
ever seen. Little does she know or care of the woes of
life. And why? Because she hasn't observed them right
from the gutter, as we have. Woe and misery!"

Gloria, sparkling all over, hoisted herself up onto
the diving board and stretched out in the sun. M'm!
Ecstasy! She squinted up into the brilliant blue dome of

the sky. Not the faintest whiff of a cloud anywhere—pure, clear, perfect, infinite. Her panting breath subsided, she breathed more and more slowly, and closed her eyes. What a nice world! What a good world!

("H'mph!" said the sad, red-rimmed eyes, never moving from their steadfast and woeful contemplation.)

Gloria stretched out her arms, sighed, relaxed, and began to practice a few runs and trills in a voice so delicate it was like a silver thread. Joy surged through her, as it always did when she was singing for herself alone. You could take it easy that way, and not have to worry over how the sound track was holding it, how your nose looked, whether your mouth was opened North-North-East or Galley-West. Tra-la-la-la-ha-ha-ha-ha-he!

The eyes looked a little less wretched. H'm! Pretty fair, that. Quite good. But she doesn't know about life the way we do.

Suddenly a shocking, brassy noise burst out from behind the wall of the pool, scattering her delicate notes like a shower of water-drops. Again it sounded, and then someone was rattling and clicking at the gate.

("There you are!" the eyes said. "That's life. See?")

"Good Lord!" cried Gloria, springing up.

The gate opened, and a warm, moist, soft young man came tripping through. "Ah! There you are!" he said. "I thought I'd find you, dear."

Gloria scowled. A fierce, angry barking rose up from the rim of the pool, where the eyes were. They couldn't stand this warm young man. Never could.

"Albert!" Gloria cried. "Stop that barking this minute."

"Burr-rurr-rurr-rurr-rurr!" said the dog, a pampered Scottie of uncertain parentage.

"Shut up, Albert!" said the warm young man.

Albert glared at both of them. If his eyes could speak! Had *he* done anything? Was it *his* fault that this awful thing had happened? It was just life, that's all. He'd seen this sort of thing in his world more times than he could remember. Hurt to the depths of his sensitive heart, Albert got up and walked away, with his tail drooping and his sad eyes dull and lustreless.

"Well!" said Gloria. "You're quite a stranger. How was the European trip?"

"Ah, cut it out, now," said the warm young man.

"Don't suppose that I mind," Gloria said. "It's all right, Jim. You don't have to come to see me any oftener than you feel like it."

"Darling, could I foresee that I was going to be so busy, so hideously busy? It's been two weeks that I couldn't call my soul my own. Three weeks. A month."

"Of course," said Gloria, lighting a cigarette. "By the way, did you hear that awful noise just before you came in? What on earth was it?"

"Now listen, Gloria, I don't call that fair."

"What's the matter?"

"You know perfectly well what's the matter."

"I can imagine there's plenty, or you wouldn't be here."

"Gloria! You know, sometimes I wonder if you really love me."

"Certainly I love you. How've you been?"

"And I love you, Gloria. I've felt terrible, perfectly terrible. But you know how it is, with one thing and another—"

"One cocktail and another?"

"One thing and another, you get all tied up and just can't see your way clear—"

"Oh, forget it. You can't seem to understand that it suits me whatever you do."

The warm young man beamed at her. "Gloria, you look splendid. I wish I could keep as fit as that."

"Well, with nothing else to do, and no worries, you see how it is."

"Of course, of course! Look, Gloria dear, I've something to show you."

"Good Lord! Not another television set! Listen, Jim, you know what happened to the last one. I want you to have the things that give you pleasure, but—"

"Nonsense, dear, television is just a closed chapter in my career. No, but just come out to the gate and take a peek."

Gloria threw a beach-robe over her shoulders. "All right, precious. Little wifie does whatever you say. If you say it fast."

He tripped along after her, moist and nervous. "Promise me you'll like it!"

"Sure, I'll love it." Apprehensively, Gloria opened the gate and peered out into the drive.

Her companion jittered beside her. "Isn't it wonderful? Isn't it the keenest number on four wheels you ever dreamed of?"

Gloria shuddered, closed her eyes, said a quick prayer, and opened them again.

No. Not a nightmare. There it was.

"Want to hop in so I can put it through its tricks? It's got a super-charger. That's what these, ah, things along the side are called. Give it more speed."

"But Jim! I bought you a car last month! I thought you had all the car you wanted with that horrible yellow thing!"

"Now darling! Are you going to rake up past history? Are you going to reproach me for a mistake I regret just as much as you do?"

Gloria sighed. No use.

"I thought you'd be pleased."

"But Jim, what *color* is it? Who ever saw a—a pink car? Or a—a—shape so kind of—"

"That isn't pink. That's salmon."

"It's what?"

"It's salmon. For heaven's sake, Gloria! Don't you know salmon when you see it? Salmon! Salmon! Salmon!"

"Oh."

"Darling, what's the matter?"

"Nothing. Nothing. Everything's just perfect."

"But Gloria, you're as white as a—as a—"

"Well," said Gloria, reeling, "that's *my* color. That's the color *I* am. Maybe it's a punk color, but it's my own anyway." With a quick movement, she opened the gate, tottered inside, poised herself weakly on the edge of the pool, and dived in.

Her husband came stamping after her—that is, up to the edge of the pool, not any farther. "Gloria!" he shouted. "Gloria!"

A sleek blonde head bobbed up from the other end. "Go away! Go away or I'll drown myself!"

"Listen, Gloria! Will you listen?"

"Go away! Go away!" The head disappeared, the water rippled over where it had been, and the pool was disturbingly free of any further sign of her. Second after second went by. No Gloria. A black fury on four legs, moving with the speed of light, came rushing straight toward the warm and jittering young man on the edge of the pool.

It was all too much. He turned and dived—not into the pool, but through the gate. Panting, he slammed it after him, while the fierce, wild noise of Albert's hunting call resounded from the other side. There was blood-lust in it.

"Burr-rurr-rurr!" shrieked Albert.

The warm young man flounced into his salmon roadster, glittering horribly in the sun, and as he stepped on the starter and slammed it into gear it jerked forward with a screech of tires.

Emerging cautiously like some timid naiad of mysterious deeps, Gloria gave a quick look all around the pool, and breathed. Safe.

But not for long. Not for a moment while these

leeches, these scorpions, these rattlesnakes could get at her. Swooping out of the pool, with the dank folds of her robe streaming and showering, she rushed over to the gate, where the savage Albert was still sounding his war-cry, snatched at him, scooped him up, and ran for the house.

Once inside, with the door locked, still showering drops of water all around her, Gloria raised her voice with all the power that had filled the Metropolitan to its topmost whirligig and echoed in the most refined and cultured ears of America. "Koko! Gertrude! Gertrude! Koko!"

A flurry of footsteps upstairs, another from the kitchen.

"Hurry!" sang Gloria. "Hurry, hurry, hurry!"

A large fat maid and a small thin houseboy appeared at the same instant, panting.

"Call the airport. Pack my bags. Get my car out. Hold Albert. Shut up, Albert. Hurry!"

"But Miss Newcombe! But Miss Newcombe!"

"Ticket for New York. Hurry up!"

"But Miss Newcombe, Mr. Wurtzberg is coming here with Mr. Rapaport and they'll be here any minute—"

"What? Who told them to?"

"Miss Newcombe, I'm sorry, they just called this minute and said they were coming and not to bother informing you because—"

"Oh. Oh, not to bother informing me. I see."

"I'm sorry, Miss Newcombe, but they said the salmon were running and they had no choice but to—"

Gloria snapped her teeth together and moved forward. "When those charming gentlemen arrive," she said, in her most harmonious and melting tones, "give them my love, and tell them I'm running too. One side!"

IV

WITH a terrific skid Moe Wurtzberg slewed his car to something roughly approximating a stop at the airport.

"Oh, my goodness!" he said, staring wild-eyed at the big Douglas tri-motor gleaming dully in the late afternoon sun, with its propellers turning ominously fast and its motors beginning to rise from a throaty chuckle to a roar. "Oh, my goodness!"

He came leaping and bumping through a motley collection of people, working his rocky elbows like a pair of old-fashioned flails at threshing time.

"Hey!" shouted a big chain-store operator, whose ribs Moe bruised with a shrewd right-cross. "What's the big idea?"

"Hi!" cried a respectable old grandmother and social arbiter, whose exclusive chapeau Mr. Wurtzberg most unfortunately knocked into a cocked hat.

"Ouch! You big bum!" gasped a gleaming and glamorous blonde, whose dainty toes Mr. Wurtzberg inadvertently scrunched.

"Well, if it ain't Broncho Nagurski!" said a rather soiled and greasy mechanic—really quite a low, rough fellow. "Yay, Bronk!"

Earnestly steaming ahead, with his eyes fixed upon his goal as are the eyes of a homeless wanderer upon

some distant shore, Mr. Wurtzberg negotiated the gangway in four wild bounces, and fell with a soft plop into
the arms of a clean-cut, uniformed official with glasses
and a stern expression.

"Stop the plane! Hold the ship! Lemme in! I'm
going!" panted Mr. Wurtzberg.

"Take it easy, take it easy," said the clean-cut official.

"Gloria Newcombe, Gloria Newcombe," said Moe in
a voice that would have touched the heart of an install-
ment collector moving in at the kill. "She's in there,
she's going, I'm going!" chanted Moe.

"Easy," said the clean-cut man. "Easy, easy now."

"Lemme in there!" snarled Moe. "Should I stand
around chewing the rag while we're losing millions?"

"Okay, Mr. Rockefeller," said the clean-cut man,
shoving him ahead. "Watch your step."

Moe stumbled dazedly through the door which was
snapped hastily open to admit him, and snapped neatly
shut after him, like the jaw of some greedy monster.

Inside the cabin, he mopped his brow and groaned
with relief. Phooey! Pretty close that time. The closest
he ever wanted to come to complete fenaglement and
frustration, not to speak of woe, misery and despair.
In a pale blur before his earnest eyes were the assorted
pates and coiffures of the passengers upon this particular voyage into the unknown, a collection of people
whom he regarded with extreme eagerness mixed with
distaste. H'm! Nobody looked like Gloria. Let's see,
now. Take it easy. That feller out there was right,
maybe he was in a pretty bad way with his nerves.

He found that he was staring into the amused eyes of a pretty young slim-Jim in a trim little uniform.

"Huh? What?" he said.

"Just one moment," she said, soothingly. "Could I get you something?"

"Wait! Wait! Listen!" he said.

"Yes, sir?" queried Miss Air Hostess.

"Gloria, Gloria, Gloria Newcombe—where's her seat, what's she doing, what—"

"I beg your pardon?"

"Now listen. Listen, this is serious. I'm asking you before this plane takes off just one simple question— do you hear me?"

"Just a moment, sir—I'll get Mr. McNaboe."

Moe peered wildly round through a haze of mounting apprehension. There was a steady hum and vibration, growing ominously greater.

"Mr. McNaboe! Mr. McNaboe, will you just step here, please?"

Moe pushed her aside and galloped frantically up and down the aisle. Gloria! What, where, how—

"Could I help you, sir?" said a grim young man in buttons and braid.

"Hey!" groaned Moe. "I've made a mistake! I'm in the wrong plane! Lemme off! Lemme out!"

The grim young man raised his eyebrows and took Moe gently by the arm. "Easy," he said. "No reason for any excitement. Everything will be taken care of perfectly all right. Just calm down, now."

Moe began to feel like some lonely, deserted wight in

a world of stern, harsh, unfeeling schlemiels who were all in a conspiracy against him.

The hostess on one side of him, the grim young man propelling him firmly from the rear, Moe found himself again at the door of the cabin and staring into the stern countenances of a group of officials who seemed to disapprove of him as a type and to hold him up to obloquy as an individual. Especially this tall feller he had bumped on his way in.

"Say, what is this?" inquired the tall feller sternly. "You wanted to get aboard the worst way. What's wrong with the ship? What are you objecting to?"

Why was it that everybody always picked on him and submitted him to all kinds of indignities and insults? They wouldn't do it to anybody else, Moe wailed. They just had a way of picking on him because—

His dim, anguished eyes suddenly grew round and protruding. Was that Gloria tripping daintily through a group of stragglers and mincing carefully up the gangway? Gloria looking as fresh and unruffled as if she had stepped out of a beauty salon after a long, intricate afternoon with an expert?

It was Gloria, all right.

"Moe! What's the idea?"

"What? What's what idea? Listen, Gloria, now you just listen to one little word I've got to say to you. For two cents I would forget I'm a gentleman. What do you mean by getting here at the last minute and throwing me into a complete nervous breakdown? Is that decent? Is that fff—"

"Hush! Calm down. Just take it easy, Moe."

"Easy! Easy! Everybody says to me, take it easy!"

"Now, now, baby, don't get excited. It's a secret. I'll write it all out and mail it to you. Good-bye."

A corps of hushed and respectful creatures fluttered around and eddied her politely in through the door of the plane, bowing and murmuring, and bumping into Moe.

"Hi! Here! Just a minute!" he said, churning along and beginning to work his elbows again.

"By gorry, Nagurski's going in again," said the low, disrespectful fellow in the soiled uniform. "Yay, Nagurski!"

"Just a minute, sir," cried the tall feller. "If you wish Miss Newcombe's autograph you will have to communicate with her by mail. We do not tolerate—"

"Gloria! Gloria!" panted Moe in anguish. "Wait!" And with one leap he negotiated the distance between them and flung his arms round her. "You can't do this, Gloria!"

"Darling, I'm sorry, I can't help it. I'll write to you."

"No, no, I'm coming, I've got my passage to Newark. Would I stay in a dump like Hollywood five minutes longer? Would I stand for insults and—"

The dazed officials began to break away. H'm! This looked like a romance. Better wire the papers ahead. A queer-looking type for an exquisite creature like that to pick, but pretty girls usually did go for the dumbest lunks you could imagine. But what about Miss Newcombe's husband? Was it true that the long-rumored break between them had finally occurred, and romance had sprouted in fresh fields and pastures new?

Gloria was whispering to this clumsy-looking cluck who didn't seem to know his own mind, if he had one. Well, too bad the loveliest star in Hollywood couldn't pick them any better than this. The hostess and the gray, stern man led them up the aisle, sighing.

Moe slumped into a low, deep chair. He would never forgive Gloria for this. In fact he would never forgive anybody.

"So I'm just an agent. So I'm just a human being. So I get pushed around, and pushed around, and—"

"Hush, darling! I'll have the hostess get you something. You're all hot and tired."

"Oh! So I'm tired, am I? And who made me tired? I ask you who mm—"

"Moe! Just take it easy. You're a perfect darling to come with me. You're a regular angel."

"To come with you? Listen, such an idea never entered my head. Such a crazy thought never crossed my brain. You pampered idols of the millions never seem to realize that we common ordinary loafers who don't make faces at sixty-thousand per have all kinds of lives of our own. We—"

"Oh, darling, don't try so hard. Just relax. This is a pleasure trip."

"For pleasure I should have six heart attacks!"

"Look, Moe, I'm in serious difficulties. You've got to help me out."

Moe groaned and closed his eyes.

"Will you? Say you won't fail me?"

"Hush, hush, let me sleep. Let me die."

"Moe!"

"Don't Moe me. Leave me alone."

"All right for you."

"Sure it's all right for me. I'm on my way to Newark to retire. I'm on my way to the old home town to curl up and die. I'm a sick man, Gloria. I got my plot all picked out in Eisenberg's Memorial Gardens. Just one thing I want you to do for me, come visit me in the hospital for old times' sake. That's all I ask."

"Huh! You'll live for forty years yet, and drive me crazy twice every year. You old fraud!"

"Gloria, from anybody else I wouldn't take it—"

"All right, baby, then just take this. Drink it slow." She held out Daiqueri Number One.

He took it, sullenly.

"Aren't you ashamed to worry me like this!"

He sipped in silence.

"Moe?"

"Let me have a little simple enjoyment, will you? How often do I get a chance? It's Moe, Moe, Moe, all the time. Newark for me."

"Of course, darling. Back to the old high school to get some education at last. Oh! Oh dear!"

Moe jumped. "What's the matter? What's biting you?"

"Listen, darling, you just have to handle this for me. What am I giving you your commission for?"

"Handle what? What is it now?"

Gloria lifted aside her voluminous furs, which had been forcing Moe further and further into a corner, but which he had not examined with any special attention. Ensconced among the sables was a strangely familiar form. Moe suppressed a loud and profane exclamation. Albert!

A pair of sad, sad eyes looked wistfully up at him.

"But they don't allow dogs on these planes. They don't—"

"Sshh! Hush!"

"Oh, my good merciful God! If this isn't the last straw!"

"Moe! Do something!"

"Should I do anything but cut my throat and bury myself in Eisenberg's Gardens? Give me a reason!"

"Moe! Albert's sick. What will I do?"

"Oh, if I were just dead and buried!"

"Listen, Moe, of all the selfish ways to talk—"

"All right, all right, give me the brute. Who cares?"

Out of his depths of woe and misery, Albert was gravely aware of great upheavals and churnings. As if the world were not bad enough to begin with, they had to take you up in the air. Down in the gutter it was terrible—but away up here in this roaring machine it was infinitely worse. Ah, me!

"There, Albert. There, baby. Moe will take care of mama's baby."

"Stop it, Gloria, stop that sickening baby-talk this instant, or you'll have me sick too!"

Albert found himself on the lap of the indignant

Mr. Wurtzberg. Worse and worse! At least he had sympathy before, at least he had understanding—but now! He had never wholly approved of Mr. Wurtzberg—found him too volatile, too easily swayed by the gusts of passing fancy. A poor anchorage for a sensitive dog with an inward agony.

The hostess tapped Mr. Wurtzberg on the shoulder.

"Sorry, sir, the company does not allow pets."

"Who, me?" said the stricken Moe.

"It is strictly against the rules of the company to allow dogs or other animals upon the—"

Moe turned up a gelid eye. "Listen, sister, I'm a quiet, refined man and I have no doubt that you mean well, but you don't know what you're driving me to."

He gave a wild look out of the window. Too late—nothing but sky. No place to go, nothing to do. *Aie, aie.*

Albert could hold his misery no longer.

"Hi! Hey! Look out! Take him, Gloria!"

"Moe, I don't know what to do, darling, I'm—I think you'd better just take him to the—"

"It's against our rules, sir. You can't—"

Moe rose up in proud wrath, and all the bottled rage and frustration of weeks burst forth. "Everybody shut up! Everybody stop heckling me! Out of my way!"

The hostess fell back; the grim young man grew grimmer. Not often was a scion of the house of Wurtzberg stirred to fury, but when he was, let everybody look out. The wrath of a rabbit is terrible; the anger of a dove is frightful.

We will now draw a thick, heavy curtain over this painful scene.

* * * * * * *

Hours later, in the blue dusk of a Kansas night, Moe was talking to Gloria in hushed, gentle tones. Upon his lap lay the convalescent Albert, exhausted and grateful. He'd been mistaken about this man Wurtzberg. He was a prince—and one of the best nurses in Albert's entire career. He'd never say a word against him; in fact, he'd never say a word against anybody. This was a pretty good old world—and as for flying! He loved it. The gutter was never like this.

"The way I look at it is this," Mr. Wurtzberg was saying. "You've got your foibles and I got my foibles, but we both of us are trying to help each other out. That's how I see it. You help me and all the time I'm helping you."

"Yes, darling."

"That's the only way to live in this world. I've found that out. Be fair to the other fellow and he'll be fair to you."

"That's right, Moe."

"You sleepy?"

"No."

"You better turn in soon. Got to keep that schoolgirl complexion."

"I'm not sleepy."

"Otherwise how do we get any more soap ads?"

"Oh! You're being practical. I thought there was a commission in it somewhere."

"Ah, forget it. It was just a crack. But listen, Gloria, I really mean what I say about—you know."

"That's white of you, darling. I won't forget it."

"Sure. You know me. Treat everybody right."

"Sure."

Gloria yawned, and gave him a sidelong look. H'm! Better watch this shark in sheep's clothing. When people talked softest, watch hardest.

"So forget about all this unfortunate salmon business—IMPORTANT never put their whole heart in it anyway, and now that they're hipped on something else, why—"

"All right, Moe. I'll forget it. Whatever you say."

"That's it. So you just take a good long rest. Go to the Waldorf, get yourself a simple little suite, relax, stay away from the telephone—"

"It sounds wonderful! Moe, you're an angel."

"Ah! Don't mention it."

There was silence between them, like warm plush. Several thousand acres of Kansas corn passed beneath them, and still not a word. Albert closed his tired eyes. A hard day in any dog's life. And Moe, looking as bland and innocent as an angel, stole a cautious glance at Gloria's face. H'm! Looked all right. Maybe she'd fall for it. He sighed, relaxed, and closed his eyes.

Still no one spoke. He breathed deeply and slowly, and his head began to nod. Minutes passed, thick slices of Kansas minutes. Moe opened one eye a crack.

Bah! He might have known. Her eyes were on him

in a hard, suspicious stare. Their glances met like two electric charges crackling across a gap, and she smiled.

"Go to sleep, darling," Gloria said.

"H'mph!" said Moe.

V

MR. THOMAS O'BRIEN, an earnest and hard-working truck-driver, was piloting his vehicle along a somewhat rocky road on the outskirts of fashionable Southampton, Long Island, and talking to his side-kick, a Mr. Schultz, who lounged in the cab beside him.

The country through which they were passing had no appeal for their jaded eyes, in spite of its fresh, green beauty and its rustic charm. You see a lot of country in Mr. O'Brien's profession; you see a lot of trouble, too. Grow gray in harness as he had, and you take your country on approval. It doesn't mean a thing.

They turned off onto a narrow, rutted road that wound quaintly through woods and fields. Birds sang overhead, happy forest creatures frisked and skipped—but Mr. O'Brien was oblivious to them all.

The truck lurched around a curve and down into a heavily wooded valley. Mossy old trees splashed them with speckled shadow; a brook gurgled and gleamed under a rustic bridge.

"Here we are," said Mr. O'Brien. "I might have knowed the guy was a nut. Livin' in a jernt like this!"

He pulled off the road onto the grass, climbed down out of the cab, and walked heavily back to the bridge. Taking a good hitch in his belt, he stepped off the road to the right, along a narrow path that wound through the trees. Or at least it seemed little more than a narrow path, so heavily was it grown with grass. Maybe it had once been a road. There were tire-marks in it where the ground was soft.

Mr. O'Brien scratched himself as he moved along through the romantic shade. Suddenly the sound of whistling impinged upon his ears. That would be Romeo. He barged along toward the sound, setting his jaw.

In a little clearing, by a makeshift old barn which seemed about ready to give it all up and fall down, Mr. O'Brien spied the happy whistler. He was lying in a hammock, with his eyes closed, while his left arm lazily moved a palm-leaf fan.

"Hey!" observed Mr. O'Brien.

The whistler opened his eyes, and smiled. "Hello," he said. "Glad you got here. I was worried."

"Yeah?"

The whistler sighed and stretched. "Smell this air," he said. "M'm!"

"Yeah," said Mr. O'Brien. "I was raised in Pittsburgh. Air don't mean nothin' to me."

"Why not?"

"Because my lungs are black."

"Are they? Well, you wouldn't know it."

"Get 'em black once, they stay that way."

"Really?"

"Yeah. So air don't mean nothin' to me."

"I'm sorry. Did you bring it?"

"Sure I brought it. What you suppose I'm doin' out here? Pickin' raspberries?"

"Nope. Wrong season." The whistler climbed out of the hammock. He was as husky as Mr. O'Brien, in his way, but he was tall and rangy instead of thick, and he had a much pleasanter and more optimistic sort of face. He was the sort of young man that girls take a second look at; they then proceed to go vague and abstracted, and forget what it is their escorts are saying.

"Back your truck off the road about half-way here."

"Say, listen," said Mr. O'Brien. "That ground's squashy. You ain't got no proper road in here."

"Sure it is. It'll hold you all right."

"Yeah? And if I get stuck?"

"I'll hold *you*, sweetheart."

Mr. O'Brien turned and strode away. The young man, beginning once more to whistle, moved dreamily towards his shabby abode. Suddenly Mr. O'Brien turned. "Say!" he said.

"What's the matter?"

"You sure you ain't gonna change your mind and send it back?"

"Send it back? Not a chance in the world."

"I've had experience with you dreamy customers that always know what you want until we bring it. So then you get sore."

"Cheer up. I designed it myself, and it's my baby. I wouldn't send it back."

"Yeah?" And Mr. O'Brien disappeared through the trees.

The young man took a key from his pocket and un-locked the wide, double doors of the barn. Swinging them carefully open, he disclosed the sleek, gleaming rear of an automobile trailer. "You beauty," he said. He squeezed himself by, up to the car to which it was attached, unlocked the car and climbed in. In a moment he had the motor going, and was backing out.

"H'm!" he said. "Lucky the weather's good. Guess the soil is softer than I thought."

It took considerable skill to back the car and the trailer along the ancient, overgrown road, but apparently he was used to doing it. In a few minutes he brought the trailer to a stop against the rear of Mr. O'Brien's truck.

Mr. Schultz and Mr. O'Brien climbed down, spitting on their hands. "Okay," said the latter.

"Isn't she a corker?" said the young man, slapping the side of the trailer. "Finest one in New York."

The trucking gentlemen eyed it sternly. They had to admit that it was a dandy article, all right. But this whole thing was a strain on them, and they clearly wanted to be off and away.

The young man opened the door into his trailer.

"Just take a look inside."

Mr. O'Brien and Mr. Schultz moved forward and peered in over his shoulder. H'mph!

"Folding bed. Frigidaire. Radio. Dining nook. All the comforts of home, and none of the complications."

"What I'm studyin'," said Mr. O'Brien, "is how we're going to get it in here. Looks pretty narrer."

"Well, we'll do our best. Can't do better than that."

"Yeah. Come on, Schultz. Get going."

They went back to the truck, and Mr. O'Brien opened up its rear. The young man climbed into the yawning interior after them.

"You haven't scratched it?"

Mr. O'Brien paused to emit a bitter laugh, and slapped viciously at a mosquito. "No, we ain't scratched it. We got all we can do to scratch ourselves. It ain't in the contract to scratch anything else."

And with the help of Mr. Schultz he unwrapped the heavy pads and blankets from around a neat, stream-lined, narrow little piano.

The young man smiled happily. "Boy!" he said. "Poppa's baby."

Mr. O'Brien restored the blankets, and attached a rope.

"One side, brother."

"Wait! I'll give you a hand."

"Do you belong to the piano-movers' union?"

"Sure!"

"Nuts," said Mr. O'Brien. "Get on with it, Schultzie."

And while the young man tugged and hauled with them, they eased the piano along to the back end of the truck.

"Wait!" said the happy father. "I'll swing around." And he climbed down and hopped into his car.

Mr. O'Brien gave Mr. Schultz a meaning look. Mr. Schultz absorbed and digested the look, and returned one of his own. Roaring and snorting, the car backed and turned until it was in a better position for the job. Mr. O'Brien scornfully attached a block to the compact little crane in the roof of the truck, and hooked the block to the rope around the middle of the baby. "Easy," he said. And they lowered it down. "Swing it now," said Mr. O'Brien. And they had it inside the trailer without the slightest trouble.

"See?" said Mr. O'Brien, breathing hard. "We got ways of doing things in the piano-movers' union."

"Gee, that's swell!"

"Sure you got it where you want it?"

"Right in the exact spot," said the young man, slapping him on the back. "Have a highball, and celebrate."

"All right, mister, but you sign this first."

"Okay. Now are you satisfied? Come on in. Make yourselves at home."

Mr. O'Brien and Mr. Schultz, considerably mollified, and soothed by the pleasing contemplation of work well done, eased themselves diffidently into the breakfast nook while their host busied himself with glasses and ice-cubes.

"Not bad," said Mr. O'Brien to Mr. Schultz.

"You said it," agreed Mr. Schultz, stretching out his large, warm hand for the frosty glass with a pleasant tinkle in it. "Here's to you."

"Check," said Mr. O'Brien. "Same to you," said their host, beaming.

"My name's O'Brien. His monicker's Schultz."

"Glad to know you. Mine's on the ticket."

"Yeah. Greene."

"Steve Greene."

"Glad to know you, Mr. Greene. Phew! Did we have a trip findin' you! Y'know, we thought you was a nut."

Mr. Greene smiled at them. "I am."

"Huh?"

"Well, sort of a nut. We're all crazy in our own way. Have another? That's right. Now, your pal here—of course I couldn't guess just what he's cracked on, off-hand, but, m'm, well, he looks kind of as though he brooded a lot."

"Mr. Greene, you said it. My pal Schultzie he broods all the time. Brood, brood, brood, sometimes it's enough to make you batty just to be around with him."

Mr. Schultz gave them a hurt look. "I got my own worries," he said.

"Sure. We all got worries. Take me, for instance—"

"You! What *you* got to worry about?"

"There you are. See?" said Mr. Greene. "Have another?"

"Nope," said Mr. O'Brien. "Not with driving. I'm seein' kind of dreamy now."

"Y'know," said Mr. Schultz wistfully as the two representatives of the piano-movers' union got up to go, "if I had some dough, and could take a good long vacation, I'd buy me one of these things."

"Me too," said Mr. O'Brien. "See some country. Go some place quiet, away from it all. No wimmin—no—"

"Brother, let me give you the secret handshake on that," said Mr. Greene. "We belong to the same lodge."

Mr. O'Brien and Mr. Schultz shuffled out.

"So long, boys. Hope I see you again."

"Sure," said Mr. O'Brien. "Huh?" he caught himself. "See us again? Not a chance. You got your gadget and you signed your agreement to keep it."

The young man laughed. "Don't worry. Nobody's going to see me for a long time."

Mr. O'Brien shoved heavily into gear. And with a happy sigh, Steve Green stepped into his trailer and looked around the neat, compact, beautifully efficient interior. "Boy!" he said, and sat down at his piano.

Letting his hands stray idly over the keys, he closed his eyes. At last! Pure bliss descended upon him, and he sighed again. His fingers picked out the vague, sketchy beginnings of a melody.

"H'm!" he said appraisingly. "Minor thirds. A twiddle in the bass. Let's see." And, humming lightly to himself, he played an experimental variation on the vague, sketchy theme. It took on a little more body, a little more color, and there was something in it that sounded as though it might develop into a delightful melody, if only just the right twist were given to it. The young man frowned, stared at the keys. "No wimmin," Mr. O'Brien had said. Only a humble piano-mover, but very astute.

"Very," Mr. Greene nodded. "I think he's got something there."

VI

IN the office of Mr. Everard Greene, President of
the old and conservative banking house of Greene &
Browne, there was a great deal of confusion. At least
there was a great deal of confusion in the mind of Mr.
Greene, and if you can say a man's mind is in his office
while *he* is in it, then there was confusion in the office
too.

Mr. Greene was an amiable, pleasant, gentle sort of
man, but on this particular afternoon he felt pretty
violent. There is one thing about the office of any man
that is not always remembered by certain people. No
matter how great the cares and responsibilities of his
job may be, there is a certain lightness and freedom
about the whole thing as long as he can leave the cares
of his home and his family behind him. A fretful wife,
an unruly child, a stern, harsh cook, a visiting mother-
in-law—all these woes fade and dissolve away when a
man enters his office and snaps a brisk "Good morning"
to his staff. They have to fade, because he is certain
to encounter so many worrisome problems at, on and
around his desk that he cannot possibly keep home and
business worries both in his mind.

Let the home cares come treading in upon the heels
of the office woes, and the result is extreme confusion.
And this is why the mind of Mr. Everard Greene was

gravely confused, not to say perplexed and distracted.

"If that woman calls again, I'm in conference," he barked into his desk-phone.

"How long a conference, Mr. Greene?" croaked the phone.

"Very long. Days."

"Yes, sir. Oh, Mr. Greene! Mrs. Greene just came in, sir."

Everard Greene raised his hands to heaven, or at least toward the chaste pine ceiling of his office. What was the use? Men weren't smart enough. Women always got at them somehow.

"Send her right in, McLeod. No one else—is that clear?"

"Yes, sir."

He leaned back in his chair and closed his eyes. If that blasted boy of his would only stop all this fooling around and be some comfort to him! Trouble, trouble, ever since he got out of Harvard. He'd been a fool to think Harvard would straighten him out and teach him some sense. Look at the professors—dreamier than the students, less practical than the rabbits, less responsible than the birds—a strange race wandering vaguely under the Cambridge elms. Could hardly expect Steve to shake off the handicap. Harvard had a way of getting 'em. Still, he was out of college now over—over eight years. Lord! It didn't seem that long.

Steve still seemed a boy. Remember when he came back from Europe with that French accent and that beard? H'mph. Got him over that pretty quick. If Steve would only settle down to business and—

Mr. Greene's regretful musing was sharply cut short by the appearance of his wife, a large, nervous, petulant beauty of fifty-two.

"Hello, Grace. Nice you came in."

"Oh, darling, I'm absolutely distracted!" She heaved a terrific sigh, and collapsed in a chair.

"I'm sorry, dear. Thought your sciatica was better."

"Sciatica! My sciatica is one of my greatest luxuries, compared to this. It's Vivian again."

Mr. Greene groaned. "I thought so. She's been haunting this office. Honestly, Grace, if you women would only remember that a man's office is a place where—"

"Oh, hush, Everard."

"Maybe you forget sometimes that I'm a banker."

"I'd hardly know it, with my income cut as it has been this season. I certainly am delighted to hear that you are still in business, Everard."

"Thank you, my dear. Some days we do business, some days we just sit and listen to the female members of our families."

"See that you do listen. Come on, darling, you can see that it's got beyond me. I've tried to keep it in my hands and spare you the worry attached to it, you know I have. But frankly, it's got me down. If Stephen would acquire just the faintest glimmering of sense, if he would just try to adjust himself to the fact that he's got a wife and a business and a hh—"

"Bah! She's not a wife. Steve can't be blamed, for that. And as for his business—"

"Yes, yes, I am perfectly aware of all the objections to Vivian. You know *I* never wanted him to marry her in the first place, and I predicted that there would only come disenchantment and des—"

"All right, Grace. All right, dear. Do relax. You're all jumpy."

"Relax! Ha! Relax! Really, dear, your humor is sometimes sadly lacking in—"

"Don't take it so hard, Grace. We'll arrange a settlement that will satisfy her lawyer, even if it doesn't satisfy her."

"Her lawyer! That man-eating barracuda. All the wealth of the Federal Reserve wouldn't satisfy his gaping maw."

"I think we can handle him. If we just relax."

"You say Vivian has been here? What does she want?"

"She wants Steve, of course. Wants to know where he's disappeared to."

"H'mph! I should like to know that myself."

"Well, so would I. I dare say he's in a safe place. In bed, possibly."

"He got his indolence from your mother. I always said so, and I'm sure I'm right."

"Bah! It wasn't the indolence he got, it was the income. Dear mother was always a little visionary about my son. That's the mistake she made, leaving him enough so that he can neglect his brokerage business."

"I always said so, Everard. I'm flattered that at last you agree with me. What are we going to do?"

"Do? Pay a quarter of what she asks, put through the divorce, and be thankful that we've washed our hands of her."

"And how are you going to get her to accept a quarter of what she wants? Really, Everard!"

Mr. Greene sighed and shook his head. "I don't know. I sit here and study it by the hour. If Steve would pull himself together and amount to something, I wouldn't care. That damn music of his! What will it ever get him? He's never sold a bar of it yet, and I don't suppose he ever will. He'd better stick to bonds."

"Oh, had he? What's wrong with his trying to be a great composer? This family could do with a little genius—especially your side. It might make up for some things."

"You're a very witty and fascinating girl, my dear."

"What is solid and dependable about bonds? Who knows what's going to happen to them? Who can tell if the market—"

"Hush! Hush, Grace! Suppose some investor should hear you? You'd start a panic."

"All right, Everard. Your humor is excellent, even if mine is not. I ask you just one thing. Refuse to see Vivian. Don't have any more to say to her."

"Thank you very much, dear. I never thought of that."

"And if Stephen should come here—"

"Come here? I haven't seen the boy in two weeks!"

"Just the same, I have a feeling. If he should, be nice about everything, please. Even if you can't sympathize with his genius, respect it. A father can do no less. Where would Mozart have been?"

"Yes. Where?"

"Good-bye, dear. Six for dinner tonight. Try to get home early."

"Good-bye, darling. Now try to relax."

"Relax!"

"Quiet, dear, quiet. Good-bye."

As the door closed after his wife, Everard Greene sighed so deeply that the papers on his desk rustled and quivered. That boy! That boy! Mozart, huh? Hell and fury take Mozart, and keep him! And Beethoven too.

He shut his eyes.

*   *   *   *   *   *   *

In the luxurious outer offices of the firm of Greene & Browne, Mrs. Greene moved in stately fashion. After all, was she not the wife of the senior member of the house, and were there not traditions of dignity and decorum to maintain?

She bowed to such subordinates as she passed in her queenly progress toward the door. Mr. McLeod, a dull, humble-looking man, rose and ducked his head to her. "Good day, Mrs. Greene, a lovely day."

"Yes indeed, yes indeed!" she murmured.

"I trust you have been well?"

"Oh, very well, very well, thank you!" she purred.

Gracious goodness, you could never get away from this man. Still, it was touching, the interest he took in her.

"We don't see Mr. Greene's family often," said McLeod. "That is—ah'm, h'r'rm—not, er—"

"Quite so, yes, yes," snapped Mrs. Greene, and turned away from him only to barge straight into the very member of the family she wanted never to see again.

"Why, Vivian, *dear!*"

"Mrs. Greene, *darling!*"

A tall, sulky blonde in an exquisite Chanel gown, Vivian pecked lightly at her mother-in-law's quivering cheek. "So delightful to find you here. I've had the worst time finding you at home!"

"Yes, yes, these servants. How have you been, angel?"

"Just grand!"

"And Stephen? How is Stephen?"

"I was just going to ask *you* that."

"Ask me, dear?"

"You know perfectly well he never sees me. Really, Mrs. Greene, I think it isn't in the best taste to remind me of the fact that I'm a deserted wife." She dabbed at her eyes.

"There, there, dear. You're still a wife, you know."

Vivian smiled spitefully. "Yes. I am. And that's exactly what I mean to be until—"

"Hush, Vivian! Not out here, before all these—"

"And where else can I discuss it? You are always strangely out, and as for Steve's father, he never comes out of conference. Does he? Does he?" she hissed, turning on the humble McLeod.

The unfortunate man jumped. "I—I—that is, er—"

"You told me he would be in conference indefinitely. *You* told me."

Mrs. Greene smiled a glittering smile. "Really, dear, I can't understand that. I've just come from him, and he wasn't busy in the least. Good-bye, dear. Come and see me."

With all the dignity and aplomb that come from a mink coat, a large income, and a fine, stern family, Mrs. Everard Greene swept out of the offices of Greene & Browne and into her waiting Hispano-Suiza.

"Home, Beattie," she murmured; and the menial eased the car gently into gear, and drove her luxuriously away.

* * * * * * *

"So you told me a deliberate untruth!" said Vivian to the unfortunate McLeod. "You kept me waiting here on the flimsiest possible pretext in order to show your piddling authority!"

"Mrs. Greene, Mrs. Greene! Please, Mrs. Greene!"

"Don't Mrs. Greene me! Out of my way!"

And sweeping the wretched McLeod aside, Vivian marched to the door of the president's office, and opened it. As she strode inside and slammed it after her, the grinning subordinates of the firm of Greene & Browne heard confused, loud noises that rose like angry ocean waves from within those sacred precincts.

McLeod snapped his teeth together and marched upon his secretary. "Hoskins! Get out those papers! Why are you idling here? This is a bank, not a young ladies' seminary at recess time. And you, Glickman. I want some action here. Get to work! Do you hear?"

The banking business resumed operations very hurriedly.

VII

ZOOMING down out of a gray, fuzzy sky, heavy with rain-clouds, the big plane came to rest at the Newark airport at an uncomfortably early hour in the morning.

Early for Albert, anyway, who was used to snoozing late in some soft and sunny nook where his dreams were undisturbed by the ephemeral affairs of the world. Albert was extremely irritable this morning; nothing pleased him, everything got on his sensitive nerves. Although he had a soft spot in his affections for Mr. Wurtzberg, nevertheless he was a little weary of him. Mr. Wurtzberg was jumpy. You couldn't rest in peace with Mr. Wurtzberg.

Moreover, Albert's stomach didn't feel good. Queasy. He was disappointed in his mistress, much as he loved her. If she really cared for him, if she were really wholly devoted to him, as she had sometimes given him reason to believe, then Albert found it hard to understand this reckless flouting of all the rules of his regimen. His diet? Completely ignored. His routine of sleep, walk, nap, siesta, walk, snooze, walk, sleep and bedtime conversation had been cruelly disregarded. It would be a long time before he would give her his absolute confidence again.

The passengers stirred themselves briskly, eager to

be out in the air, rather than up in it. The usual subdued clamor, punctuated by sharp noises of greeting,
rose about the plane. There was rather a crowd, particularly for so early in the morning. There was, especially, rather a crowd of those frowsy, scraggly, oafish
individuals customarily employed by journals of large
circulation to annoy people of importance or notoriety
upon their arrival at any given destination. These latter
individuals proceeded to crowd about Gloria immediately upon her appearance in the harsh, drab light of a
Newark morning.

Albert and Mr. Wurtzberg found themselves on the
outskirts, very much to their annoyance. What a de-
pressing place! thought Albert. Ah! Newark! Newark!
thought Mr. Wurtzberg, as the aroma of the Jersey
flats came subtly to his eager nostrils. After all, you
could travel anywhere, but you couldn't find another
town like Newark.

"Thank you, gentlemen, thank you," Gloria was saying, in her sweetest voice, which was sweeter than the
honey of Hybla at any hour of the morning. "But that
is all I can say. A picture? It's such a thrilling new experience, I can't resist it."

"Is it true that you have definitely *phhhht*, Miss Newcombe?" asked one ill-shaven fellow with a drooping
hat-brim and a hard-bitten pipe.

"Ah, ha, ha," Gloria laughed. "How could anybody
imagine that there could ever be any misunderstanding
between Jimmie and me? You're so funny."

"Would you care to comment on your rumored romance with an unnamed gentleman who accompanies you on this trip, Miss Newcombe?"

"There's nothing I'd like better, but I'd hate to blast your illusions," said Gloria. "And now I'll have to hurry. Thanks for talking to me. Good-bye!"

"Hey!" said Moe. "Take it easy, baby. Don't forget your pals."

"Thank you so much for being so good, darling. I suppose I won't see you again for ages. But I'll never forget what you've done for me. Come, Albert."

"All right, all right, I'll tend to Albert. We're doing fine, Al and I are. Just go slow, or you'll be a nervous wreck one of these days. Look, Gloria. Newark!"

"Wonderful! Marvelous!"

"Want to see the old high school?"

"I'd love to, darling, but I think I'd just better go to the Waldorf for now."

"Okay, Miss Glamorous. Is it true that you are contemplating the severance of marital relations with that low-down, no-account, good-for-nn—"

"Moe! Don't you talk about him. Are you taking me to the Waldorf, or do I take myself?"

"Of course I'm taking you. Would I leave Albert like this?"

"So sweet of you, dear."

"Glad you appreciate it."

He led her to a big black sedan. A uniformed chauffeur stood at frozen attention. There were initials in gold on the car door. Little Abe Fancher's initials.

Gloria's lips lost their long curve as her eyes went to Moe.

"Sure it's Abe's car," he admitted. "A favor to me. You don't mind riding in it, huh? It's a good car."

Gloria permitted herself to be persuaded. The motor began to purr.

Albert gave a soft, low moan. The machine age! He was about fed up with it. Bang! Bang! Roar! Roar! That was the way the world went nowadays.

"Here! You hold Albert for awhile. Give him some baby-talk. He looks as though he needed it."

"Oh, poor Albert! Come."

Gloria fussed and fondled the gloomy and misanthropic graduate of the gutter, while Mr. Wurtzberg spoke softly to the driver. The car started.

"Did you tell him the Waldorf? The Waldorf, chauffeur."

"Where would I tell him? Honestly, Gloria, sometimes I wonder if you trust me."

"Oh, I trust you all right. I trust you fine. Gee, Moe, I'm tired. All this has been too much for me." Gloria leaned her head on his shoulder.

"Go to sleep, baby. Oh, look, look! Newark Fire Department."

"Goodness! Do they know you're out? Wave to them, Moe."

"Hi, boys! How've you been?"

"Oh, look, Moe! Newark rain. It's coming down in buckets."

"Naturally. We give you the works in Newark."

"That's where you learned the art, is it?"

"Go to sleep, now. Don't spoil your voice."

"All right, darling. Gee, what a trip. I wonder why I came. Do you remember?"

"Not me. Go to sleep."

"Moe, you're horrid."

"Shhh! Take it easy. That's the girl. Easy now."

"Don't you say easy to me."

"Shhh! Shhhh!"

*   *   *   *   *   *   *

Whistling happily, Steve Greene parked his car, with the glistening new trailer behind it, in front of the skyscraper where his father's banking offices were located. It took some doing to ease into the space available, but luckily the morning traffic was not at its peak.

Squaring his shoulders and shoving out his chest, Steve marched in through the bronze doors of the executive offices. Now for it. He didn't know just what kind of a reception he would get, but the old man had never let him down, and he didn't think he would do it now. Great to have a father like that.

The moist, amorphous countenance of McLeod greeted him from behind a capacious handkerchief, immediately after a rather violent sneeze. Thus Steve's entrance was something of an anti-climax, going more or less like this:

"Kuff-whush-phfff-morning!"

"Howdy, Mac. Better take care of yourself."

"Huh-huh-hhh-hh—"

"That's all right. I'll just bust in on the old boy. Want to surprise him."

Steve opened his father's door and edged himself inside. "Good morning, pop. How's business?"

Everard Greene choked on the aspirin tablets he was just on the point of swallowing.

"Phfff-ff-m'gg—"

"Well, so you've caught it too. Charming, charming."

His father waved wildly toward the water-cooler.

"Oh! Wants a drink. I get it. So the great barons of finance converse by means of wind signals now. A new kind of inflation, h'm? Here, here, drink slow now. Don't be greedy."

Everard Greene gasped, shook his head, leaned back in his chair, and sighed.

"How are you, pop?"

"Don't ask me that."

"All right, I never said it. As for me, I never felt finer. Feel that muscle. Here, slap me on the chest. Come on, put your weight into it."

"Go away, go away. Grow up."

Steve sat down opposite him. "All right, sire. Sorry."

"Your mother and I were up all night talking about you."

"Come on, don't try to overwhelm me with compliments."

"Where have you been?"

"In the woods."

"I thought so. How about sticking to your job?"

"Now look here, pop, whose career is this, yours or

mine? I've been working harder than I ever did in my life before. And another thing—I've no intention of staying in the brokerage business and I never led you to believe that I had. It was all your idea and I only made a half-hearted effort at it to please you, or rather to show you that it just wasn't my line and never could be. There's only one thing in the world that I care a damn about and that's the thing I'm going away now to work on. You can't stop me, and you'd better not try."

"Music! Music! Fooling around with all those queer sharps and flats. Now look here, Steve—"

"Music is the word, and it's the final word, too. So long."

"You stay right where you are. I didn't set you up as a broker just for ff—"

"Now come, pop, you know it's illegal for you bankers to mix yourselves up with the stock market any more. I thought you'd learned your lesson. The world moves. Times change."

"You're a bright, smart boy, aren't you?"

"That's high praise, from you."

"Your mother is worried sick over you. All this Vivian business—"

"I'm sorry about that, pop. It's got me down, but how can we help it now? I'll figure something out."

"She hounds me."

"She wants money. She doesn't like us."

"My money! I don't see you making any."

"All right, it's not my fault that I'm a rich man's son. I never wanted to be. Remember one thing, that she'd never have been interested in me if you hadn't been there with your blasted money. That's all she was ever after—I was just an incidental nuisance. An off-stage noise."

"I sent you to Groton. I sent you to Harvard. I sent you to Pp—"

"Well, I'm going one place that you didn't send me, and it's about time. You and your money can go—"

"Get out of here!"

"Some day I'm going to pay you back every cent you've given me, and be under obligations to you as a man, not as a pocket-book."

"You can do as you please about that."

"Ah, listen, pop, take a couple of weeks off and come along with me. I'll give you a great time."

"No."

"I'll do the cooking and messing around. All you'll have to do is lie around and let your whiskers grow. You'd make a damn handsome tramp, pop. You've got the real stuff in you if you'd only let it come out."

"You shouldn't have said that about my money."

"I know it. I'm sorry."

"I hate the stuff too, but your mother—"

"Sure, I know. You're a regular guy, the best there is. Only, don't you see that I can't just go and make the same mistake? If I'd taken that brokerage business seriously and really worked at it, I'd have had to give up the thing I was born for. And I won't do that, pop."

Mr. Greene sighed, and shook his head. "I don't know much about music, but I know whh—"

"You know what you like. Sure, and so do I. I'm not asking you to like it, I'm only asking you to give it a chance. I've wasted half a dozen years puttering around with charts and seasonal indices and all that junk. It drives me nuts. I hate it. One morning I woke up and decided it was better to be real, not an imitation. And that was the day Vivian lost whatever faint interest she had in me. Maybe I'll be a tramp. I don't know. But I'll be a real one."

"I liked that song you wrote last January. Whatever happened to it? I thought you had something there—maybe."

"I threw it away. No good."

"H'mph. The careless genius."

"I wasn't careless enough to leave it lying around. Well, are you coming with me? What do you say?"

"Steve, stop it. Don't get me thinking about it. Don't say another word."

"Listen. I just want to tell you about it."

"Steve!"

"First, my idea is to get away off so far from this dizzy city that I'll never remember there was such a place. How would you like that?"

"Steve!"

"I thought you would. Then secondly, I plan to . . ."

*　　*　　*　　*　　*　　*　　*

"Wake up, Gloria! Here we are!"

Gloria stirred and sighed. "Draw my bath and lay out my bathing suit. Oh! Oh dear!"

"We won't have to draw you any baths, kid. And you won't need the ocean."

Gloria rubbed her eyes. Overhead there was a steady beat, beat, beat of rain. She stared out through sheets of it, and shivered. "Oh, darling, how terrible!"

"Forget it. Here's the doorman with a nice big umbrella. Hold on just a second till I ransom you."

Clutching Albert, Gloria ventured forth into the driving downpour. Vague, fleeting shapes slithered and bumped their shadowy way through a strange, washed-out world. A tall flunky in uniform guided her into a stately-panelled lobby, with Moe damply skittering after.

"*Aie, aie,* baptism at last. What would my father say?"

"Oh! My luggage!"

"Don't worry, don't worry, it's okay, we'll take care of everything. Stick with me now. It'll be over in five minutes."

They were entering an elevator.

"Five minutes? What do you mean?" Gloria stared around her. "Moe, you've made a mistake. Where are we?"

"Now, now, don't get excited, baby. Tenth floor. Take it easy. Some old friends waiting to welcome you, that's all. Just a little formality."

"Moe! I'll run out on you! I'll—"

"In this rain? With your delicate constitution? Gloria, listen to reason."

"I know where we are! You're taking me to Abe Fancher's office. I'll never speak to you again."

"Listen, I'll never speak to you either if you let me down. How would I feel?"

"Moe, I don't want their old contract and I told you so. If a girl can't depend on her agent, who can she—"

"After all I've done! And this is gratitude. Bah! Albert is grateful, anyway. Aren't you, Al?"

Gloria relapsed into a wooden silence. Very well. Let them heckle her all they wanted. It would do them as much good as ever. She marched stiffly along to the offices of IMPORTANT PICTURES, INC., without deigning to cast a glance at her perspiring companion.

A reception committee of minor executives was waiting, all smiles and sunny enthusiasm. "Good morning, Miss Newcombe! How nice to see you here in New York! Wonderful of you to come all this way. Mr. Fancher will see you at once."

Gloria set her teeth. "You bet he'll see me."

A rotund, cheerful, happy little man burst out of the inner office. "Gloria! Moe! What a surprise!" It was Little Abe himself. "Come in, come in, come in! Have a couple of cigars, Moe. Sit down, Gloria. What'll you have?"

"Make mine a lemon," said Gloria. "You have wonderful service at the Waldorf."

"Now, now, don't get mad. We were all worried sick over you. Listen, Gloria, what does this mean, you don't want to take part in the greatest and most educational epic IMPORTANT has ever produced? I thought we saw eye to eye on things."

"Did you?"

"We realize that an artist of your standing has more than the usual amount of temperament—"

"Not temperament. Temper."

"Temper? What's wrong with that? It's one of the most valuable things in pictures." Abe could be almost completely convincing at times. "But listen, Gloria— have you seen the script before you say no?"

Gloria put her foot down sharply. "No, Mr. Fancher! Isn't it enough that you want to ship me up to Alaska to watch a lot of silly fish swimming up a river to end in a cannery, with me doing the canning until some bearded hero comes along and discovers that I am Gwendolyn Pitty Puss, the missing heiress? God's whiskers, man! I am a singer! I've got to sing or sink! I understood I was to get operetta, and all I get is fish!"

"Gloria, you're tired—you've been working too hard," Little Abe cut her off. Spreading oil on troubled waters had long engaged his talents. "Why not go to the mountains for a few days? Run to the Adirondacks —use my camp at Sand Lake. Get rested, get a new outlook on life. You can hunt and hike and fish— No," he amended quickly, "you don't have to fish. Just forget all about this story. It don't mean nothing. You know we can always change the story. That's easy! IMPORTANT will do anything to please you, and to prove it, I hand you a new contract at *three* times the old figure." He drew himself up dramatically into five feet two inches of solid generosity. "You heard me, Moe? You heard me, Gloria? That's money I'm talking, not cigar coupons. Well," he beamed at Gloria, "what do you say? If you don't want to go to Alaska, we can switch the story to Oregon—"

Gloria shook her head in a decisive no.

"I'm sorry . . . really I am. But it isn't your geography that frightens me. It's what you are doing to me, Mr. Fancher!" She flashed a nervous glance at the door. Story changes! She had heard that before. She wanted to get away; to be through with all this nonsense.

Abe stared at her aghast. "Do you mean—think of the money!" he shrilled.

"Don't you dare bully me with your money!" Gloria shot back. "You've locked me up with wiggling mackerel and pushed me out of airplanes. Now you want me to can salmon! Why—why, if I signed that contract you wouldn't draw the line at making a—a—strip tease girl out of me! I tell you I'm through! I can't stand it!"

"Gloria! Wait! *Wait!*"

In one swift motion she snatched up Albert and leaped through the door.

"Stop her, Moe! Moe, keep after her!"

"Gloria, Gloria, come back! Wait!"

Rushing wildly through a scattered flurry of minor executives, secretaries, clerks and office-boys, Gloria gained the elevator just as a flunky was emerging with her overnight bag. Snatching it from him and darting into the elevator, she hissed to the startled operator, "Quick! Quick! Close the door."

"This is an up car, lady."

"Close it! Close it or I'll set the dog on you."

"Okay, lady. It's agin my orders."

"All right. Down!"

"Listen, lady—"

"Down, I said."

The car started down.

"Step on it! Don't dawdle!"

The ornate doors of the elevator crashed open. Disheveled, distracted, Gloria darted out into the corridor and towards the street. People stared after her. The doorman jumped aside. "Taxi? One moment."

"Moment me no moments!" cried Gloria, and dashed out into the rain. Dimly, in her wake, she heard confused sounds of pursuit. Desperate, she stared this way and that through the rain.

An empty trailer stood at the curb. Quick! Try the door. Good! Not locked. This was escape! With a rush she darted inside, to pile up on the floor, her hat hanging over one ear, her clothes awry and Albert snorting his disgust.

She caught her reflection in a mirror and she had to look twice to be sure that this was the great Gloria Newcombe, late of the Metropolitan and much later of Hollywood.

"Albert, this is marvelous!" she sighed. "Now if the owner of this contraption will pull it around the corner, we'll slip out, and—who knows—maybe we'll send Moe a post card from Paris!"

VIII

SHAKING hands with his father, Steve started out of the office.

"Well, if you change your mind, you know where you can reach me. Don't forget!"

"Nonsense, nonsense! Wouldn't think of it."

"So long, pop!"

"So long—"

Turning up his coat collar, Steve peered through the rain. Rotten day to start out on, at that. Wonder how it would be to hang on for a while till this foul weather blew over. Gusts of rain splattered against the windows; while outside dark, wet, gloomy shapes hustled for cover or trudged soggily on.

"Doad cash tchcoad," said the moist McLeod, and exploded into his handkerchief like a tired bombshell.

"Thank you," said Steve. "Same to you."

"I—h-huh-hhuhh—"

If he stayed, though, it would mean more Vivian. Also, there'd be just as much rain here with Vivian as there'd be anywhere else. I'll take my rain straight, Steve said to himself—and opened the door, and ran for it, while the wretched McLeod exploded behind him with a hollow boom, like the last salute in some dim, damp war.

Snapping out his keys, Steve locked the trailer door,

hopped into the car, mopped the rain out of his eyes, and set the motor going. Stay in New York? He guessed not! Now that his decision was made, he felt extraordinarily gay. Whistling happily, he swung up Broadway and across to the Drive.

*   *   *   *   *   *   *

Albert was furious. What kind of treatment was this? After all he had done to make clear the simple fact that he disliked social life intensely, loathed offices, and wished to meet no one whatever at any time! Insincere, two-faced people who were as likely as not to shut you up in a closet with the brooms and leave you there! And as for rain, he had indicated his abhorrence to it time and time again in the most unmistakable manner. So now what did he find? He found all his cherished beliefs in his mistress rudely shattered and ground to bits. All he had ever asked from her was sunshine, warm weather, a few cushions, and porterhouse steak. Surely that was little enough! Surely he was not demanding too much from the woman he loved!

And now, this silly dashing hither and yon, this hectic and undisciplined quest for the amusement of the moment, the glitter of the bright but tawdry dream!

Was it right? Was it fair? Was it defensible from any point of view whatever? He thought not. He most certainly thought not.

Albert was willing to admit to prejudice. He freely granted that he was fallible in his judgment, like any dog. He claimed no supercanine prerogatives or ca-pacities. But he did demand justice. To him justice was as dear as the bright pp—

Gloria wrapped a handkerchief tightly around his jaws. That would keep him from barking until she was safely out of here. Wouldn't do to risk being found out.

"Albert! Sit still! Stop writhing!"

If looks were words, if glances were nouns, verbs or adjectives, what would Albert's eyes not have said at this juncture?

Gloria crouched nervously on the lounge, not daring even the narrowest peep through the drawn curtains. Those vultures! Those bloodhounds! A fierce exulta-tion surged through her. She'd shown them! And on top of showing them, she'd made the neatest getaway in the history of these United States.

Let's see now! Should she ride a few blocks, wait for a stop-light, and hop out?

The rain slithered and swished against the windows of her tight little sanctuary: it drummed on the roof like the hoofbeats of a pursuing army. She looked appraisingly round. H'm! Not bad. Nice and neat, anyway. Glad whoever she was with was a person of refined tastes. She'd stick for awhile, and figure out what to do when the time came. The beauty of being in here was that she didn't have to bother about the problem of what to do or where to go—just let every-thing slide, confident that the farther this accommodating fellow took her, the harder it would be for those buzzards to find her.

She hugged herself with joy. She would have hugged Albert, but he disdained her fickle caresses and slunk away to sulk in a corner. He was through with women. No more toying with him.

How about taking a ship for Europe? She stretched out on the lounge to think about it seriously. M'm! Paris. And swarming visions came of little grey streets, shabby old courtyards, noble avenues, horse-chestnut trees, the Dôme, the Champs Élysées, the Opéra-Comique, where she'd always wanted to sing, Rue St. Jacques, the chimney-pots along Rue de l'Université, the gowns in Rue St. Honoré, the food every-where. . . .

Gloria sighed deeply. There was a game she often played with herself, which was to decide where she would live when she settled down. It had always re-mained a game, for in order to settle down one must have something more than annoyance and frustration to settle with. Her unfortunate marriage, which had lasted only a few months and had been entered into out of a mixture of pity and boredom, had more or less soured her on the subject of domesticity. Still, she never saw Jim except when his allowance was running low. If only he had a mother, or a couple of fond old maiden aunts to fuss over him. For, he'd never got past his fifth year. His simple, sunny delight in toys of all sorts (as long as they were big, shiny, compli-cated and expensive) was one of his most endearing qualities. As long as you didn't have to pay the bills. Give him a new camera, an amplifier, an enlarging machine, a lathe, an outboard motor, a car, two cars, a yacht, and he was as sweet as he could be for as much as a week, often two weeks. Nobody could be sweeter than Jim with a shiny new gadget.

Men were feeble, childish creatures. Now take women—they had a lot more strength of character. Women took things as they found them, and—

"Yip!" said Albert.

Gloria leaned over and reached wildly about, seeking him.

"Shhhh! Albert, you bad dog! Do you want to ruin me?"

Albert scowled at her from his dignified and solemn retreat in the darkest corner. The handkerchief, in neat shreds, lay at his feet.

"Albert! Come here!"

If eyes could convey the apotheosis of negativism, that is the kind of negativism Albert's eyes would have conveyed.

Gloria reached in and got him by the scruff of the neck. "Poor baby, I hurt his feelings. Come, pussy. Come, baby."

Pussy! Baby! It was insults now. Albert would have the world know that he had no connections of any sort whatever with the despised feline race; moreover, that he was full-grown, mature, and of settled and conservative views.

"Come sit in mama's lap."

No mahatma could have perched with greater austerity upon that delectable spot. Albert looked grimly at the teeth of the piano opposite him, and bared his own right back at them.

Patting and stroking the obdurate and unforgiving dog, Gloria let her mind wander down some of the streets she had known in Paris, like a lonely, eager adventurer seeking a home. Rue du Dragon . . . Rue des Acacias . . . Quai d'Anjou . . . Avenue d'Iena, Rue des Quatres Vents, Avenue President Wilson . . . noble streets, shabby streets, rich streets, poor streets . . . the fine dignity of Rue de Grenelle, where she met Marshal Foch out walking when she was a little girl, and he bowed and smiled at her . . . the jolly bustle, the busy clacking excitement of Rue Daguerre at supper time, when all the housewives were busy cooking, or running out for a few extra inches of bread, or a bargain at Félix Potin's. . . .

Gloria sighed, and closed her eyes. Albert edged himself a little closer. So he was getting some of the attention he deserved, at last! True merit was coming into its long-deferred reward. Well, he was willing to consider the subject of restored diplomatic relations. He wasn't hard. Over a juicy porterhouse steak, which no doubt would be forthcoming at the usual hour, he was willing to discuss their mutual misunderstandings and difficulties.

The steady movement of the trailer, the faint vibration and the occasional slight jouncing of the springs, were all very soothing to the nerves of Gloria and her companion. To Gloria, they meant absolute safety as long as they lasted. To Albert, they meant an excuse to snuggle up to his mistress without giving himself away. Of course a walk would be fine, but as long as it was raining—

Albert prepared himself for a good, sweet snooze. Gloria dreamed about Paris. . . .

*   *   *   *   *   *   *

Just as well I took a bum day, said Steve to himself. Less traffic. He kept a steady speed ahead, feeling a little like the pilot of a boat. With luck he might make it before dark. Let her rain!

Too bad the old man wouldn't come. Do him good to get away from the job for awhile. Poor old chap, with those women on his neck! Steve made a wry face. What a swell world it would be if all the women would just go and take a jump for themselves into space, and stay there. They were up in the air most of the time anyway.

Or if that wasn't practical, why not invent some kind of a box you could shut 'em up in? Equip it with all the gadgets they liked, stock it with provisions, give 'em a new hat every week to talk through, supply 'em with gossip to keep 'em happy, stick all the boxes together so that they could monkey with each other's business, build a fence around the whole mess a mile high and forty thousand miles around, and let 'em stay there. The men with sense could take the rest of the world; the ones who hadn't any could visit the reservation until they got some.

After his experience with Vivian, Steve felt that he could get along fine if he never saw another woman for fifteen years. Used to think they were pretty swell, but he guessed that was just his inexperience.

Now you take pretty girls. From the time they're able to walk around and say "Goo" everybody tells them they're sweet and lovely. Little boys fall all over themselves to run errands for them, sharpen their pencils, hold them up on their skates or their bicycles, and what do they get for it? A sweet look. When the little darlings grow up all they have to do is just hold their faces in a good light and wear a wistful expression and they can be as selfish, thoughtless, bad-mannered, ill-tempered, mean, grasping, and underhanded as they please. And what do *they* get for it? They get all the best things in the world, that's what they get. How could a really beautiful girl ever find out about the tough spots in life? She's shielded from them all along the line. Nobody can bear to see *her* tired or hungry or in trouble. Forty dreamy-eyed men leap to her aid whenever the smallest thing goes wrong.

"Pretty girls? Bah!" said Steve. The ugly ones were the only ones who had the faintest glimmering of compassion or understanding. Scratch the surface of the beautiful ones, and you scratch all.

You know, there'd be some swell fishing up at Sand Lake. Perfect season for it, weather would probably be right too. Ah, what a break to be able to relax at last and be sure he'd be alone! No women within miles of where *he* was going! Wonder how the bass were striking.

He speeded up. Peekskill . . . Poughkeepsie . . . ought to make Albany by noon.

Of course he was really going to work when he got there—but you've got to relax too, haven't you? Certainly! The beautiful thing about these arguments you carried on with yourself was that you always were sure of a fair hearing for both points of view. And no screaming. No weeping, either. How do they turn it on? he wondered. Must be some kind of a special gadget they have. And boy, how it works!

Better stop and get something to eat soon. Guess he'd duck into a bean wagon; that would be quicker than messing around in the trailer. Anyway, he wouldn't want to break in his new gasoline stove on a mere highway, with all these damn billboards and *You Eata* signs around. He'd dreamed of lighting it up for the first time out under the sighing, aromatic pines, with the wind coming fresh over the lake and all the stars for company. No stars tonight, probably, but there was one good thing about stars. You knew they were always there, even if you couldn't see them.

Ah! Here was a likely-looking place. *Joe's Diner.* Steve pulled in to the curb.

*   *   *   *   *   *   *

Gloria rubbed her eyes and sat up. Well! So the chauffeur had stopped at last. Now for the explanations. Better give these people some money, thank them for the lovely ride, and go to a hotel until she had figured out what to do next. The trouble with a hotel, though, was that somebody would probably recognize her. Too bad the trailer just didn't keep going all day. Oh, well, she never had any luck.

She snapped open her vanity, and dabbed on a little powder. Then she fished out a pair of enormous smoked glasses and put them on. All ready. Let 'em come!

Minutes went by. Nothing happened.

She went cautiously to a window and drew the curtain aside just a crack. Wonder what town this was. Didn't look like much. Joe's Diner, huh? What a miserable little place! Gloria couldn't imagine what sordid pursuits went on in such a low dive—did people actually eat there? She wouldn't be surprised if they served food that came out of cans, monstrous as the idea seemed. H'mph!

You know, it must be almost lunch time. She patted Albert sympathetically. "We'll have to do something about you, boy."

Albert pricked up his ears.

"But just what, I swear I don't know." Gloria felt a little thick in the head. She knew she had to make up her mind about all kinds of important things, and it was necessary to make it up very soon. But she was groggy from fatigue, and all she cared about was getting some more sleep, years of it. Lucky she hadn't gone in for crime. She'd never be able to live up to the strenuous demands of such a career. At the very point where it was necessary to execute a brilliant coup (whatever that was) she wouldn't be surprised if the cops didn't find her curled up somewhere with neuralgia or the megrims. How did these smart desperadoes ever keep their affairs straightened out? They'd have to keep a card index of their various undertakings, with the necessary steps in each case neatly catalogued. And as for the lies they had to tell, the disguises they had to wear, the arrangements they had to make, the elaborate getaways—

Gloria sighed. Lucky there were no cops after her. She had that to be thankful for, anyway.

What was eating this fellow, anyway? He'd been in this repulsive place for ages. H'm. Guess it was he who was doing the eating. Poor Albert.

A greedy person, her unknown companion must be. After all, there was a limit to everything. Maybe there were several of them, and they were in there whiling away the hours with gay, insouciant banter and light badinage, while she and Albert grew gaunt and wasted with famine. The pigs!

Let's see, now. Had to figure things out. They'd be coming back any minute. Gloria concentrated with all her might. She had read once in a psychology book that the best way to remember anything was to let yourself drift off into a state of abstraction. Let yourself go limp, relax all your muscles one after the other, make your mind an absolute blank, and—

"Wurrp!" Albert said.

Gloria came to with a start. Gee! Almost went to

sleep that time. Now let's see. What had she been thinking about? Oh yes, a blank.

But why a blank? she wondered. Let's see, let's see.

Just then two round, bulging people, a man and a woman, came out of Joe's Diner. Gloria jumped back from the window and crouched on the floor. Here they came! She trembled with excitement. The woman had a kind face, anyway. She couldn't tell about the man, because he seemed to be mostly spectacles and whiskers. They reminded her a lot of old Aunt Emma and Uncle Ted, out in Arizona. Well, she was safe with nice, simple elderly people like that. Maybe she could persuade them to take her along with them for a few days, until those pirates had given up the chase and found somebody else to pick on. Mightn't be a bad idea. Gloria got up from the floor and sat down on the piano bench. She could feel at home in this little cubby, with nice people like that to look after her. The piano would come in handy, too. She heaved a deep sigh of satisfaction.

If they'd only hurry up and find her! They looked as though they'd dined altogether too well. Really, for old people like that to be so greedy! It didn't look nice. Cautiously, Gloria crept to the window and peeped out again. The stout couple were standing by the curb, arguing about something. She let the curtain fall and jumped back just in the nick of time. Didn't they know enough to come in out of the rain?

She was debating whether to tap on the window to attract their attention, when she heard a car door open and shut with a sharp thud and felt a slight jouncing of the springs run back into the trailer. Thank heavens, they'd got back in, and she wouldn't have to bother with explanations for awhile longer. Honestly, she was having miraculous luck. Now she could just relax again and forget about the whole thing. She curled up on the lounge, sighed, stretched, and closed her eyes. Good old Aunt Emma and Uncle Ted! Hadn't seen them for years.

Really, Albert thought, this was getting to be too much. It was about time he used sterner tactics. "Yipe!" he remarked sharply.

"Albert! Albert! Stop that!"

Albert glared. What was this? Who was doing the remonstrating here?

"Burr-rurr!"

"Albert, if you don't stop this instant I'll put you out in the rain. Do you hear?"

All Albert's proud Scotch ancestry, as well as his more dim and problematical lineage, rebelled in wrath. This wasn't cricket. It wasn't even football.

The car started with a jerk. Albert missed his footing and bumped against the piano bench. Baring his teeth, he snapped at one of the legs. Let 'em all come after him! He'd show 'em how they did things in California.

Gloria began to explore the center of the trailer, where the kitchen seemed to be.

"Just you wait, boy, I'll fix you something or bust."

Stupid of her not to do something about it before.

After all, why should anybody mind? She'd pay handsomely for the kitchen privileges, when the reckoning came.

She opened some cabinet doors. Whee! This was much better than she could have dreamed! Provisions of every kind, rows and rows and rows of them! And here was the neatest, most ingenious little refrigerator she'd ever seen. And food! Good Lord, look at the food! What greedy people! What darling, angelic people! Look, Albert!

Albert's eyes glistened. Poetic ecstasy surged within him. All the cares of his long, sad life fell away from his shoulders, and he felt a younger, stronger, better dog.

Gloria bent over and studied the handsome little gasoline stove. This ought to be easy. She knew all about stoves. What you did was turn a hicky here, twist a hicky there, pull out this, push in that, adjust this gadget under that rod, move this thing over a bit, release the catch, twist the screw, open the vent, pump this little plunger, warm up this horizontal pipe, feed this burner—

Ouch! Oo!

Let's try again. Procedure A. Holding the handle of the plunger with one hand, gently turn gadget XV3, release catch AR9, and then, with all the self-control and fortitude at your command, adjust pin Bk11 and apply a match to—

There was a faint pop, Gloria jumped a foot, treading on Albert.

"Urroo!" said Albert.

A sweet, sickish odor, as of escaping gasoline, permeated the interior of the trailer. Gloria felt a little faint.

Opening a narrow little door, she peered inside. Ah! A bathroom. She turned on the tap, and bathed her face well. Then she let the water run on her neck. M'm! She felt better.

With a baleful glint in her eye, she set to work on the stove again. Was a Newcombe going to let herself be licked by this? Certainly not. Turn handle, release plunger, breathe hard, adopt slightly stooping posture with little finger of left hand pointing due N and instep of right foot carefully poised between toe and heel. Exhale.

His eyes watering, his nose quivering with anxiety, Albert watched her. Ah! Success. A beautiful clear flame appeared in the burner; a radiant smile spread over Gloria's features, like dawn over a lovely landscape.

How good life was! Now for the porterhouse steak.

Gloria rummaged about. Let's see. This looked like something. Opening a compact little package, she disclosed two neat slices of fresh, pink salmon. Salmon!

"Ipe!" Albert said, leaping forward. The idea of dropping his porterhouse steak! Still, he could eat it just the way it was. H'm. He sniffed at this unfamiliar food. Dim, buried memories stirred within him. Smelled familiar. Some rare delicacy he'd enjoyed long ago in his youth. This was more than he had hoped for. Wriggling with gratitude and eagerness, Albert wolfed, or, rather, dogged the two slices of salmon in six hearty gulps.

Something to be said for this strenuous life, after all. It sharpened your appetite, refined your perceptions, made you savor the richness of things. After all, you got in a rut if you didn't look out. Maybe a little travel was good at that. Broadened you. Albert licked his chops, and wagged all over. Good Gloria. Nice Gloria.

Leaning weakly against the piano, Gloria stared straight ahead of her. Fate, that was it. Some malignant, ugly, fat old demon had worked a charm on her and there was nothing she could do about it any more. What was the name of that fish-god in Paradise Lost? Dagon. She wouldn't be surprised if he were mixed up in this somewhere. All her superstitious Pennsylvania upbringing began to tell on her. Hexes. Witchcraft. Three times round the bamberry bush, eenie meeny minie moe.

Moe! She shuddered, and closed her eyes. Goodbye, everybody. I'm done. I'm through. It's just meant to be, that's all. I'm going to signal Uncle Ted and Aunt Emma to come in and get me.

But I'm going to make a fine, attractive victim at least. Nobody's going to say that the corpse was in the slightest degree disheveled. On the contrary, I'll be the finest corpse that's ever come out of a bandbox.

Peeling off her dress, she lurched and swayed into the bathroom. There was something voluptuous about all this beautiful soap, these luscious big towels, and these wonderful shiny gadgets. Oh, for a shower! She squinted round at the elaborate little contraptions that seemed to bristle everywhere inside this amazing vehicle. Sure enough, there was a shower, and it had the most dainty and finicky curtain you could imagine. Goodness, Aunt Emma had nice taste!

Gloria stepped out of the rest of her clothes, and turned on a faint, delicate spray. Better hurry, as the water supply couldn't be very great. She stepped under the shower, and shivered with pleasure.

Suddenly she skidded, and fetched herself a clip on the ear with the soap. Uncle Ted was turning into a reckless driver lately. Must be doing over sixty. Lucky she was in top form, or she'd never be able to keep on her feet. Propping herself up, she bent over so that the spray could douse her back. M'm! Again she slipped, and this time bumped her head against the wall. Hey! Put out your hand when you're going to stop, you big brute!

She waited for awhile to see if Uncle Ted would steady down, but he just seemed to get worse and worse. The trailer was constantly stopping and starting, and the worst of it was, it didn't do either gently, but it jumped. If there was one thing Gloria detested, it was jumpy driving.

Moving to a window, she lifted the curtain and peeked out. Oo! Right in the center of a big town. More than that, right in the center of vision of a startled traffic cop. For one electric instant, she stared straight at him, and he stared straight at her, and then she dropped the curtain.

Whoo! Better give up this luxury stuff and get back into some clothes. Suppose it had been Uncle Ted, coming back to the trailer for his pipe, or something. Picture his chagrin at seeing her in such a state!

Gloria turned off the shower, hustled into her clothes, snapped off the gasoline stove, which was just wasting its sweetness on the desert air anyway, if you called it sweetness, and sat down to get her ideas straightened out.

The best thing to do was attract the attention of whoever was driving this thing so insanely, tell some kind of story, say good-bye, and get out of here.

Still, might have some lunch first. She *could* open a few cans. As a general rule, of course, she didn't approve of canned food, but sometimes there were perfectly justifiable exceptions.

She looked over the cabinet of provisions again. After all, Fate couldn't make salmon out of everything. There must be other things here. Sure enough—tomato juice, soups of all kinds, spaghetti, beans, sweet potatoes, bananas, dates, spinach—really, there was every kind of food you might wish for, if you weren't hankering for crepes suzettes or baked Alaska.

Alaska! Well, guess there was no ducking that topic after all, so she might just as well make the most of it. She busied herself with a few choice samples of Aunt Emma's provisions. This time she got the stove working at once. Guess things weren't so bad after all. She heated up some onion soup.

H'm! A bit pungent, what with the smell of gasoline and soap, not to mention Albert, but it would do. At least it reminded her of Paris.

She sat down in the dining nook to eat. Really, this trailer wasn't at all bad. She'd always been a little captious of the things, never having been inside one before, but it took only a little experience to convince her that there was a great deal to be said in their favor. No agents around. No telephones. No husbands. No contracts popping out at you from behind a palm frond. Nice rain on the roof, to make things cozy. Think of poor old Moe running around and getting wet, looking for her. She grinned. Still, she hoped the poor darling had his rubbers. Wouldn't do for him to catch his bronchitis back.

Well, she'd certainly shown them that she was cleverer than they were. So now she could afford to be tolerant and sympathetic. After all, they meant well.

"Here, Albert. A little milk for you. Drink slow."

If Uncle Ted would just smooth out his driving things would really be very pleasant. Wonder what that traffic cop was thinking about.

Better not try to imagine.

Gloria looked round to see if this wonderful trailer had any more contraptions that would be fun to play with.

Why, a radio! What fun! She sighed with pleasure. **Really, it was too bad about poor Moe, worrying** about her, probably raving and swearing himself sick by now. She must send him a post card or something.

Guardedly, she turned the radio on. There ought to be some helpful hints about tatting or beauty treatment about now. Funny about radio programs, they were so terrible during the day that it must be a different race of people who thought them up. The thing was, they were intended mostly for women. That was why they made them terrible. Gloria didn't think much of men or of the way they treated the female sex. If she had her way there would be a law passed about men.

She listened lazily to the music that came in. The orchestra had a cold, or something. There was rheumatism in the air. She turned the dial.

"Have YOU seen these filmy creations executed by Tweedie Sisters' EXCLUSIVE mercerizing process which is warranted to retain all the dainty charm of . . ."

She tried again. H'm! A news broadcast.

"Berlin. Phewrer Hitler calls for increased budgets for airplanes. Entire male population of Reich to be placed under arms. Means no harm to France or to the rest of the world, the Phewrer declares. Palo Alto, California. Herbert Hoover, in an interview today, declares that the policies of the present administration are undermining the liberties of the people. . . ."

Gloria reached forward to turn the radio off.

"New York. Gloria Newcombe, the singing star of IMPORTANT PICTURES, disappeared mysteriously this morning after a conference with the president of the company. No possible reason for her disappearance can be imagined except foul play, says Mr. A. B. Fancher, the president. 'We will leave no stone unturned to run down the perpetrators of this colossal crime,' Mr. Fancher declared. J. Edgar Hoover has placed his G-men at the disposal of the frantic picture barons. A kidnapping for ransom is the reason ascribed for Miss Newcombe's disappearance. All highways are being scoured by the State Police. Further bulletins will be issued over this station. Your announcer, Keith Witherspoon."

The wolves! The brutes!

Gloria jumped up and began pacing the floor of the trailer. Trapped! Hunted! Haunted! Hounded! What should she do? What could she do? Was there no way to escape? She leaped for the door. Locked! She lurched back to her seat, sat down, and buried her face in her hands. What was the use? They'd get her some time, so they might as well have her now. All right, she'd make an uproar and get Uncle Ted and Aunt Emma hopping back here.

Yes, and give herself up to some hulking cop? As far as that went, get poor old Uncle Ted into trouble? Whoo! What a mess! Her head was dizzy. Wearily, she hid her face in a pillow.

*   *   *   *   *   *   *

There was something puzzling Steve. Every once in a while, he had the queer notion that he heard a dog barking. Whenever it happened he would cock his head and stare all over the highway and among the trees. No dog.

H'm! Funny. Hadn't had a drink in a week, so it wouldn't be that. Was his mind becoming unhinged from all the worry and vexation he'd been through with Vivian? They claimed the first sure sign of mental trouble was the hearing of "voices." Oh, to hell with it. Maybe something was wrong with the transmission or the universal joint. A slight buzz at a certain speed, which sounded like a dog. Stranger things than that had happened to him, lots of times. Offhand, he couldn't recollect what they were, but he was sure there had been plenty of them. Down on the farm when he was a kid, for instance—the way the old house had creaked at night, and the sound of groans coming from under the stairs. The sighing of the wind in the boughs of the ancient trees around his father's estate, the mournful noise of the mill-wheel turning—sure, there were always lots of funny sounds going on, and if you were a little keyed up and the situation was just right, you interpreted them as something else until you found out exactly what they were.

He'd give the car a thorough going-over in the morning. Meanwhile, keep the speed up. Weather seemed to be clearing a bit, anyway.

There weren't many towns to hold him up any more. As the afternoon wore on and the miles rolled smoothly under his tires, the country became more and more rugged and wild. Silvery lakes gleamed dimly through the rain, rimmed with feathery trees. The car had to do some climbing on the hills, but Steve kept it to a constant sixty, and higher when there was a good stretch. Not much competition to worry about any more. This was the way he liked to drive.

Through his head, the little melody he had stumbled on the day the piano had been delivered kept running over and over. Every once in awhile he would whittle off a couple of notes to make it more compact, or try it over to see if he couldn't shine it up a bit. The elusive element it needed was hiding now very close at hand, like some tiny creature whose gay song you hear in the stillness of a summer night, so faint and far away that it is just on the border of hearing, not quite distinguishable from the sound of the wind, the rustle of leaves, the trickling of water.

Steve drove on in a trance. Then there were other things weaving themselves through the little melody —his ideas about women, for instance. That subject stuck somewhere in his head and he couldn't get it out. It kept bumping into the thread of melody and getting all tangled up with it. Money, too—he was bothered about that. The whole business of money and what it did to you and the people around you; the dirty gouging you had to do, the squeezing of little people who couldn't fight back because all they had to depend on was their jobs. If they lost their jobs, they lost everything.

H'mph! The nobility of being poor. The dignity of labor. Some of the sweet old millionaires he knew didn't allow it very much dignity.

"I'd like to write a song about that sometime," Steve said grimly. "A fighting song."

He stared ahead through the misty drizzle. Trees were a hell of a lot better than people—much cleaner, and a lot more dependable. He'd take trees any time.

Hi! Have to watch himself on these curves. That truck had almost run him down. For a hundred yards, Steve slewed all over the road. Better stop dreaming and stick to the right side of the white line.

Damn it, there was that dog again.

He shook his head violently, and rubbed his eyes. Better get himself a tonic of some kind. All this mooning and brooding was taking its toll.

> *You take wine,*
> *I'll take song:*
> *You take women—*
> *I'll get along. . . .*

Forget that for awhile. Polish up the melody later with the piano. Stick to business now.

Say! Something queer about this road. Didn't seem familiar, somehow.

Good Lord, am I lost? Steve peered all around. No route signs for miles.

He'd swear he'd never seen this old mill before. Still, there was something like some place he had seen somewhere, sometime, about some of it.

> *You can fool some of the people some of the time,*
> *And you can fool*

Some of the people
Some of the time,
But you can't
Fool
Some of the people
Some of
The
Time!

Nuts! Take it easy, now. Let's see. H'm. No place to ask, no place to go. No place to yes, no place to no. . . .

"I guess I'd better send for that tonic right away," Steve said. "First it's money, then it's women. Next it's dogs, and now it's doggerel. Cut it out, you tramp. Keep your mind on the road."

Yes, he was lost, all right. This wasn't the route at all, even if he'd seen it in his childhood or maybe in a dream. Well, have to turn back, that's all.

Steve waited for a likely place to turn, and started back. No songs, now. No dogs, either. Keep your head clear. Retain a stiff upper lip. Brush your teeth night and morning, see your dentist twice a year. Face the world clean-limbed, clear-eyed, unafraid—

There was that damn mill again. Quaint. He stepped on the gas.

Ah! It was where that truck had come barging at him that he'd got rattled and taken a wrong turn. Just like his own life, you know, when you came to think. of it. He was doing fine and whizzing straight ahead just the way he'd wanted to go, and then Vivian bore down on him.

Wrong road ever since.

Well, he was going to fix that. Just give him a couple of weeks to think things out, get a few songs under his belt, catch a few fish, do a little visiting with his fine old friends, the trees, and maybe he'd get on the right track again. You bet!

IX

GLORIA was as brave as anybody. She had been over most of the world and done a lot of things, so she didn't begin to quiver and get mousey when things became a little scary. Her method of dealing with trouble was to stand right up to it and knock its teeth down its throat. But as darkness closed in more and more and the great rugged hills grew more wild and strange, she felt a little uneasy.

There is something about the woods at night, something about the weird, still, dim gloomy trees . . .

Something cold and lonely about a lake with the dark clouds heavy over it, no stars out, no sign of a moon. . . .

Gloria had been peeping out very often lately. The disturbing thought had come to her some time ago that maybe those two nice old people she had seen standing by the curb weren't the owners of this trailer at all. She'd just assumed they were because there wasn't anybody else around when the car started.

Wasn't there? She concentrated with all her might. Had she seen either of them get into the car? No, but she hadn't seen them walk off down the street, either. Because she had ducked out of sight and hidden for several moments.

"You *are* a prize moron," she said to herself. "What

on earth were you thinking of? Didn't your mother teach you better sense?"

She smiled ruefully at that. Poor mama, with all her fussy little instructions about everything under the sun, from the proper way to put away the soap after you used it, to the correct behavior at a cotillion! She'd be surprised to see her daughter now. The angel! Gloria wished she had her right here. Or even better, that she were back in the green Pennsylvania hills, with their friendly, gentle contours dotted with smiling farms . . . back in the old house with the shades pulled down, the doors all locked, and a jolly big dinner on the table. . . .

"Come on, Newcombe," she said to herself. "It's just these wild woods, that's all. You won't find any Fascisti among them, like that time in the Alps you almost got shot prowling around over the fort. Well, how should I have known it was a fort? There wasn't any sign out."

She hugged Albert, and crouched against the wall, looking out through a narrow crack in the curtain. Wonder if she'd ever been in this part of the country. Maybe when she'd been a little girl. Well, she didn't like it. Next time she'd pick a better chauffeur.

Brrrrr! She shivered. Maybe he was a gangster. Maybe he was in the fish business.

Heavy, black and thick, the night closed down; the car sped on deeper and deeper among the somber hills.

After awhile it turned off onto a narrow dirt road, and from then on, for what must have been more than an hour, it followed rude, bumpy roads that were sticky, wet, and soft as pie. The driver went into second, then into first. The wheels spun, the motor roared. They moved onward, with a slewing motion like that of an inebriated elephant on a skating rink.

Once they got stuck in a ditch. Gloria felt like a worm letting her unknown guide do all the prying and shoving necessary, but she thought he would hardly be in the mood for an exchange of social pleasantries, so she cowered inside with the angry Albert. Albert was worrying about dinner; Gloria was worrying about how she could steal a look at Uncle Ted without being seen. Her plan now was to wait until they had definitely arrived at whatever place they were going, and then, while Uncle Ted was busy over some little chore or other, just sneak off by herself to the nearest hamlet. That would be as neat as anything. What connection with New York would she have then? Just turn up innocently at a nice, quiet country inn, ask for a nice, quiet, comfy room, say hello to the folks, introduce Albert, and go to bed for a week. Perfect!

Silly to have been so frightened.

Cautiously drawing a curtain aside just a crack, she peeped out. But the man was entirely out of sight. She tried the other side of the trailer. Smack against a fuzzy spruce; nothing visible.

"I'll bet he's swearing. And who wouldn't be?" She listened to the heavy clunk of a stone on mud. H'm! No swearing that she could make out. As a matter of fact, he seemed to be whistling.

Pretty soon he climbed in, and the motor roared again. Good work, Mister Uncle! They were slewing again.

Every couple of miles, now, there would be one of those lonely little houses that are so characteristic of American country, and of no other on earth. No little warm clusters of towns, with the village *place* where the people congregated to gossip and have a drink or two—just the gaunt dark hills, the great spaces of a vast land, the little lonely houses. Out West Gloria had been so overwhelmed by that isolation, that stark aloneness of her countrymen—the enormous spaces in Wyoming, Texas, Idaho, the forlorn settlements, so soon lost in the vastness of prairie, mountain and desert.

"Come on, stop feeling so sentimental," she told herself.

Albert wished *he* had some space to walk in.

Suddenly the car stopped by one of the little hamlets she had been brooding about—a small, pale, bare wooden box set down right against the road and left there.

Gloria peeped out. And this time she was rewarded by the vision of a very tall, wet, muddy man, with hat pulled down and coat collar pulled up, who stepped down abruptly and went and pounded on the door of the little pale box.

Her heart, which should have sunk, leaped. She felt it give a little jump, there was no mistaking it. The light from inside the house shone on his face. Young!

She strained her eyes. He was gesturing toward the

trailer, obviously with pride. Out of the house came a little old fellow with an extraordinarily spry, jaunty step. She heard the vague murmur of their voices, without making out any words. Anyway, the spry fellow liked the trailer—she could see that. In fact she saw it just in time to hide herself. Her heart beat painfully, but after a few moments she was able to breathe comfortably again. They had apparently come to some understanding; grandpa nodded his head brightly many times, the tall young man slapped him on the shoulder, and was back in the car once more.

Off they went, this time over a road so villainous that Gloria was determined to write to the *Times* about it, when she found out where it was. Maybe they didn't get the *Times* out here.

They were following the wide, long curve of a lake shore; she could see the water glimmering faintly through the somber pines. Virgin forest, this—it made her think of Indians. The Indians made her think of bears, the bears of wolves, and other unidentified but extremely unpleasant creatures that slunk and snarled at you from the dark, and crept after you when you walked trembling on.

Albert growled.

The road turned off again; they lurched, slipped, bumped, skated, and stopped.

The driver climbed out. She heard his footsteps coming toward the trailer door. In a panic, all her fine plans whirling dizzily away like so many scraps of paper into some obscure scrap-heap of the mind, Gloria seized

Albert and, lifting the lid of the lounge, crawled ignominiously into its depths, scraping her nose and giving a sad twist to her knee.

A key turned briskly—the man came in. He did not hear the thunderstorm of Gloria's heart.

She could see his shoes, the bottom of his trousers. They were soaked with mud. Look here, my dear, this is the stupidest thing you've ever done in your life, Gloria told her cowering heart. Come on out and speak your piece.

Yes, but which piece? Her head throbbed with pain and confusion.

She peeped out. The man was taking off his clothes.

Discarding the selection of speeches, Gloria crouched back under. If 'twere done when 'tis done, 'twere best it were done quickly. Albert was squirming. Up his throat she could feel a growl coming. She squeezed him close: the growl came out: she screamed.

The bare feet of the man appeared to leave the trailer floor. Perhaps the floor was sinking, though. If only she were sinking with it!

A startled face appeared at the lower edge of the opening: Gloria was just poking hers out: their noses met.

"Ow!" Gloria said. This was their introduction.

"What's the matter?" asked the young man. "Are you in trouble?"

"My nose," Gloria said. "Oooo!"

"Better come out," said the man.

Of all the cool young customers! Gloria felt herself

getting mad. After all her plans, too! Spoiled, all of them! Any minute now the whole story would be out.

"Excuse me for, ah—for undressing, ma'am, but I didn't know I had a lady accom—accompanim, ah—"

Ha! He wasn't cool. She could see his hands shaking. Gloria smiled.

"I was just going to take a bit of a swim."

Suddenly he stopped apologizing and got mad. Apparently what he had said so far had been just a reflex, what any gentleman would say in the circumstances. If ever in them, of course, which wasn't likely.

"Who are you, how did you get in my trailer, and what's the big idea?"

Albert acted. He'd had enough, Albert had. All the bitterness and frustration of this long, inhibited day spoke in his bristling body. He hurled himself upon the angry young man.

"Hi!" said the angry young man.

"Albert! Albert! Down! Down!" shrieked Gloria.

Albert yapped a surly yap, and flung himself out through the trailer door. The great open spaces for him.

"I'm in a jam!" Gloria faltered. "Don't get angry. I'm sorry. If I'd known it was someone like you driving this thing I'd never have got into it. I mean—"

"I see," said the young man quietly. M'm! So handsome!

"Oh, I didn't mean that—you see—"

"This thing, indeed! I'll have you know that there

isn't a job to equal this on the whole continent of North America. This *thing!*"

"Yes, yes, honestly, I like it. I love it. But you see I—oh, for goodness sake stop standing there in those ridiculous—shorts of yours and trying to look dignified! I hurt my nose on your floor, too."

He found himself a bathrobe in a closet apparently stocked with clothes.

"A woman!" he growled. His glare was something fierce. She had never seen eyes which could blaze so. What a singularly unpleasant young man! Some spoiled brat, with lots of money to waste, who knew nothing of the world and would fall all over his feet in a drawing room. Gloria stared coldly back. She wished she had her black spectacles, though.

"You'd think you'd seen a—a snake or something," she snapped.

"Lady, I've seen snakes. I'm an expert on all kinds of snakes, particularly on the poisonous specimens which infest this region, but never, in all my—"

Snakes? Poisonous? Gloria felt suddenly small, cold, and strange. The dark world around her seemed to swoop up enormously into towering, menacing forms. "I want my mother," she said (but not to him). "I dislike you extremely," she said. "Stop it!"

He bristled. "Oh! So you tell me to stop. I see. How interesting! Well!" He sat down. "Won't you, my good woman, be seated?"

"A gentleman doesn't sit down before a lady!"

"Bah! I'm no gent. I'm a tramp. Gory Gus, dat's me."

"I could have told that without your interesting help," Gloria said. She was tired and fretful and wanted her dinner. Pâté de foie gras, artichokes en beurre, quails on dry wheat toast, green salad with roquefort, and mama. . . .

"Well, I'm going for a swim," said the young man. He looked very tired now, as if all the joy had gone out of him. And so happy when he came in! Gloria was simply furious. This was absolutely the first time in her life that any man had ever been so completely overwhelmed with gloom, not to say disgust, at seeing *her*.

He barked a question at her suddenly. "From the Carioca Club? I thought so."

Gloria jumped. "Don't shout at me!"

"Just a question. Technique. The way the detectives do it. I've watched 'em."

Steve was thinking as quickly as his vexation and confusion would allow him to. There was this Carioca Club, the usual kind of night spot—he'd noticed it in the basement of the old man's building any number of times. Some dizzy wench who'd got too close to a customer's wallet, probably. Very sweet, very nice. Women!

"Speak up, can't you? I won't bite. Get mixed up in some trouble in the Carioca Club?"

Gloria nodded. Now why am I doing this? she asked

herself, in wonder. Look at me, saying yes to him already. Are we mice, or are we women? We're putty.

"Sure, I run outa the Carioca Club," she said, twisting her mouth sideways and trying to look tough. Wonder if the accent is right. "The cops were after me an' my pals." Pals? Now why had she brought pals in? Wasn't it bad enough already? Get started on a lie, and she never *could* keep her head clear.

"You an' your pals, huh?"

"Yeah."

"Come on, speak English again. Relax. You don't have to act. You obviously haven't got the talent." He grinned at her.

Gloria stiffened. Then she grinned too. "All right. But really, you can believe me or not. It's true. I did sing there." (Sing there? Gloria, can't you stop it?)

"I believe you." He smiled again. "I hope you'll overlook my bad manners. I was startled, that's all."

"Of course. I'm sorry to have spoiled your swim. I was in such a jam I just had to seize the first chance to get away—I've been hidden all these hours, and now I—"

What is this? Steve said to himself, way down where nobody could hear. What am I doing? Is this dancing school? Is this Princeton? Is this Yale? The horrid thought brought him to. Hold 'em for Harvard. Also, hold 'em for God's sake.

"Look here," he said sternly. "I don't know what you've done, or what you're capable of doing. Judging from your appearance I'd say it's plenty. But I do know this—that I came all this way just to work, and enjoy a little quiet fishing, and that's what I'm going to do. Why you came here I dare say we'll find out when we read the headlines."

He got up and started out.

"In the meantime, I trust you are familiar enough with the interior of my trailer to make yourself at home in it. Lucky for you the name of this road is mud. You can stay the night. And for your information, my father, my grandfather and myself are all eagle scouts in splendid standing. I shall sleep in the car. Of course, I won't mind." His sarcasm was meant to be killing. "In the meantime, you may roam through the spaces of this compartment as freely as you like. Only for the love of Mike don't get my lines tangled up or drop hooks in the soup. Now I'm going out." He was in the bathroom, apparently getting into his bathing suit.

Gloria closed her eyes. Well, here it was:

"And in the morning, my dear girl, you'll have to go."

He came out, bowed to her, and strode away through the door toward the lake.

"Can you cook?" he shouted from twenty yards away. "I'll bet you can't."

"No!" shouted Gloria into the murky dusk. "I can't!"

She sat down on the cushions and began to cry. Fishing!

Lord, it was dark here. The trees seemed enormous, like the kind of trees you dream about as a child, in some enchanted wood where knights and giants live, and dragons go smoking and flaming. Why should virgin forests always be so dark and huge? You'd think it would be more appropriate if they were made of little, dainty trees, birches maybe, or silver poplar, the kind with those tiny twinkling leaves.

A terrific clamor suddenly started up somewhere close at hand. It was the voice of Albert, barking like mad.

"Burr-rurr-rurr-rurr-rurr-rurr-rurr-rurr!"

Gloria jumped up and ran to the door. No use; the woods were too dense. Anyway, she needn't have bothered, because a swift lump of darkness came hurtling out of the gloom, and darted past her into the trailer, whimpering. This was Albert, the undefeated champion of Wilshire Boulevard. This was Albert, hiding under her skirt and complaining in a little voice. Somewhere out there in the darkness was Albert's master.

"What was it, boy? A wolf?"

Albert whined and growled. "Wuff!" he said suddenly. He leaped up and stood at the threshold, his nose advanced a quarter of an inch into the menacing and quiet night.

"Burr-rurr-rurr-rurr-rurr!" Meaning, I'm not afraid of you, you blackguard! Come in here and fight!

Gloria laughed. "That's the boy." She was suddenly illuminated with an idea. Going quickly to her forgotten overnight bag, she opened it. She was positive that she had put something in here that would teach that rude, uncouth and repulsive young man a lasting lesson. Ah! She smiled to herself. This would shame him. She took out a shimmering dinner gown of powder blue—

the only thing in the bag except for a few scattered accessories to beauty, and a pair of pajamas.

"All right, boy, you guard the gate," she said, and closed the trailer door. Albert, encouraged by this, let out a loud, harsh bark that would scare anything.

"All right, boy, you said it. Now you can take it easy." She hustled out of her rumpled dress, and into the dinner gown. Ha! Manners! She'd show him manners.

This gave her another idea. Cook, could she? Out of the way, Albert! A woman's honor is at stake. She had forgotten all about her plans of the afternoon. Let 'em wait.

She was busily lighting the gasoline stove. She was as good at it now as an old hand. It worked like the ideal of all gasoline stoves, the ultra-stove, the stove of stoves.

She rummaged swiftly among the stores of food. He could have the rest of the onion soup. Ripe olives, anchovies, hearts of artichokes. Coffee. H'm! A regular sybarite. Well, here were some simpler things. She got quickly to work, and in a few minutes had a supper steaming on the stove.

Albert wagged his tail, and kept stumbling over her feet.

"Wuff!" he said.

Let's see, now. Anything else she could do? She wandered to the front of the trailer. The door of his clothes closet stood open. She peered inside. Shabby old trousers, spotted jackets, boots—what a dandy he was! And then her eyes fell on a fine expanse of black. A dinner coat! She did not hesitate an instant. She reached in and got the coat, vest and trousers, and laid them neatly out on the bed that wasn't a bed. Ha! Lord Chesterfield would get a gentle hint when he next favored her with his presence.

Where would the shirt be? She scurried around, found one in a drawer, as well as studs and links and tie, laid them all out, and purred with appreciation of her own cleverness.

Look, Miss Wonderful, it's all right to amuse yourself and your charming new friend, but how about your little problem? Oh, bother the problem! There was a faint rattle on the roof—seemed to be getting ready to rain again. She crouched down beside the radio and snapped it on. After all, it wasn't every day you heard 'em asking for you like this.

She fiddled with the dial. No luck yet. Well, naturally they wouldn't be asking for her *all* the time. She busied herself with the supper. H'm! Nice dishes he had. Octagonal Wedgwood, as delicate and fine as ivory. What kind of a tramp did he call himself? Only millionaires or freaks would bring dishes like this into the wilderness.

Suddenly she spun around. MOE!

Oh, heavens! Oh, my gracious Lord! It was only his voice. For a moment Gloria had thought she was going completely off her head. Over the radio were coming the earnest accents of her old guide, counselor and double-crosser, Moe V. Wurtzberg, in person.

"And this reward of $5000 I personally offer for information leading to the arrest and conviction of such person or persons as have fiendishly abducted Gloria Newcombe. All America waits anxiously to hear news of her. I personally am waiting with the greatest anxiety. It is indescrib—"

A few yards away, the sound of happy whistling. Galahad was returning. Quick! Quick! She snapped Moe viciously off, ran to the drawer where the knives were kept, snatched up a paring knife, and while her host was actually fumbling at the door, cut the wires of the set in one neat swipe, close to the wall where they would not be noticed—she hoped.

Galahad was knocking. "Hi! Hey! Hi in there, Miss Floor-Show!"

Gloria strode to the door and opened it. She stood there, smiling effusively. "Good evening. Won't you come in?"

The tall young man stared at her.

"Come in, *do* come in!"

He did, without a word. Staring dazedly round he came face to face, or at least face to dish, with the food. He stepped back, stumbling over Albert. In order to avoid Albert he swooped over to the folding bed, almost sitting on his dinner shirt. This time he stood perfectly still.

"Dinner will be served when you are dressed, sir."

"Huh?"

He turned and stared at Gloria. She looked primly at the floor.

"Ha!" he said.

"I will leave your repast to simmer while I saunter," she murmured, in her most dulcet tones. "Come, Albert." She stepped outside, with Albert rather reluctantly at her heels, and closed the door.

Oo! A big wet raindrop. Oh, dear! She opened the door of the car, and got in. Albert was right with her. No more walks for Albert—not tonight.

*   *   *   *   *   *   *

Over their demi-tasses, served in the delicate Wedgwood cups, Mr. Stephen Greene, of the Harvard, Racquet and Savage Clubs, and Miss Gloria Newcombe, of the Metropolitan, dallied lazily. Between them, stuck firmly into saucers, two candles burned. The soft sheen of linen shirt-front and of powder-blue satin gave grace and dignity to the occasion; their voices were appropriately low, their accents well-modulated.

"Won't you tell me more about your music?" Gloria cooed.

"Won't you tell me more about yours?"

"Oh, it's nothing to compare with yours! I wouldn't speak of it in the same breath. You know all about me now. A couple of appearances at the Carioca Club every week, and the rest of the time a home girl, in my tiny nest on Hudson Street."

"Hudson Street!"

"Certainly. Over a garage."

"I see. An all-night garage?"

"Yes, with the big trans-continental buses coming in for overhauling and refueling. M'm! I lie awake for hours, just listening."

"I see. Sounds wonderful. Look, I believe you—that is, about some of it. I think your voice gives you away. I'd know you were a pretty good singer from that."

"Thanks very much."

"Sure! I can't be fooled about voices."

"Oh. You can't."

Steve got up. "Shall we go to the music-room, Madame la Comtesse?"

"Mais je suis éblouissée!"

"Me too. Would you like to hear something?"

"Yes, of course. What is so delightful as to relax after dinner to the dainty strains of some Debussy tone-poem?"

"Debussy! I hate him. Neurotic squeals and moans, then he goes boom, crash! So powerful. You'll be asking for Tschaikovsky next."

"I certainly will not. I'm asking for Greene."

"H'mph! That's better."

"Play one of your—shorter compositions?"

"My compositions are all short. Should a poem go by the yard?"

His hands began to wander over the keys. He sighed. Good tone, for a little dingus like this. He smiled at her. "Like my piano?"

"It's cute."

"I designed it."

"You're cute too."

"H'mph. I dare say." He played one of his more conventional songs. She talked all right, but you couldn't expect her to know too much. A certain kind of sleek, smart woman could always appear to know the latest and best of everything, no matter what, if it was a subject for polite after-dinner conversation. No matter how distinguished a man was in his field, even if he was a great authority known all over the world, these bright women never hesitated to talk right up to him, and what was the worst of all, to talk back, to argue, to disagree.

Bah! Women! He broke off abruptly.

"What's the matter? I liked it."

"I'm sure you did. I picked it so you would."

What was the matter with this man? Something seemed to be biting him, nibbling away at him all the time. Another one of those tragic get-away-from-it-alls? How dull, if that was it! She thought that had gone out of style by now. So much of it a few years ago, all those gloomy post-war boys coming out in repeated rashes of reminiscence, and sitting spectacularly round afterwards, away from it all where the tourists could see them.

"I wouldn't mind singing some of your stuff," Gloria said.

Stuff? Some of his *stuff?* Steve smiled coldly. "I'd love to have you sometime." He got up from the piano and sauntered over to the radio. A night-club gal, and she wouldn't *mind!* "But I don't want to bore you with that kind of thing. Let's see if there isn't something a bit more popular here." He turned the radio on.

Gloria fidgeted. "Oh, but I'd love to hear more! Please! Really, I liked it ever so much. I think you have very good possibilities."

Possibilities? *Possibilities!* Steve glared at her, and then glared at the radio. *Now* what was the matter? No current? He fiddled with the dial, turned the set round to peer at the tubes. H'm! More trouble. First it was the universal joint barking like a dog. Oh! No, the universal was all right. He knew where the barking had come from now. He glared at Albert. Running off to get away from his family, especially the female members of it, and look! A regular domestic mob! Absolutely stuffy with comfy domesticity. Stuff, huh? Possibilities, hey? Wouldn't mind, hah?

He turned and smiled at her. "By the way, we haven't said anything about the particular crime for which the police are interested in you. After all, I'm sure it's more interesting to you too than any possibilities latent in my music. What did you do?"

"Do? I won't tell you."

"I thought not."

"You're an extremely bad-mannered young man."

"Am I?"

"Yes, you are. I'd like to know who brought *you* up."

"I'll see that you're introduced."

"Thanks very much, but I'm afraid my social engagements wouldn't permit it."

"At the garage, you mean?"

"Certainly, at the garage."

"At any rate, you may as well face the fact that whatever your trouble is, it might very well catch up with you, and you'll have to take steps to return to your garage in the morning. This is an adventure in contentment, not a kidnapping or something."

Gloria's heart jumped.

"I offered to listen to your story, indeed to be of help to you, but apparently you won't trust me with it. Well, that's your affair."

"I told you I'd got in a jam at the Carioca."

"What were you doing there in the morning?"

"It's a night club!"

"Oh! I see."

"When would you expect me to be there, nine o'clock? That's my bed-time."

"Your bed-time? Oh, excuse me. I'll leave you to your dreams. If you dream the cops are chasing you, don't scream, please." He opened the bed for her. It *was* rather tricky.

He snatched some pajamas from his wardrobe. "Good night to you, Miss Mystery."

Really, this man was impossible. "Good night to you, sir. Thank you for a charming evening—and charming treatment!"

He went out, slamming the door.

Gloria made a face at it, just as it opened again. He laughed. "Pretty, pretty! There's a bolt in the door. See that you use it."

"Good night."

"Good night!"

The door slammed shut.

"Wurr-rurr!" said Albert, right at it. Gloria shot the bolt with a click.

And he'd left the dirty dishes! The oaf! Gloria flounced to the bed, opened her overnight bag and snatched viciously at her pajamas. Such gallantry! Such consideration!

And after all she'd done to make the evening charming. Men were always rough, thick-skinned, unimaginative, dull, possessive, overbearing, clumsy, gross, and stupid!

I hate men! I hate them, I hate them, I hate them!

She snatched off her beautiful gown, and snatched on her pajamas. She fired the gown into a corner, and crawled into bed. Then she had to get up to snap off the lights. There was a sudden swish of rain, and a wild, sharp rattle on the windows. The roof sounded like a thunder-storm.

Well! What a beautiful picnic! Imagine coming out into this hideous wilderness in weather so utterly horrible! The loon! She huddled under the covers. The uncouth lout!

She yawned. Outside she heard the dull, heavy music of wind in the pines, like a weary undertone to the staccato voice of the rain. Far off, an animal sent up a weird, lonely cry. Albert growled, and crawled up on the bed.

Wonder how he was doing out in the car. . . . He'd be uncomfortable. He was so tall, he'd have to wind himself up and tie three knots. Well, how could she help it? He'd insisted on it. Not out of gallantry at all, but out of sheer distaste for her company. And Chanel had made that dinner gown, and named it after her, too!

Served him right.

The rain came down harder. A harsh glare lighted up the cracks in the curtains, and there came a crash of thunder. Gloria pulled the covers over her head.

*　　*　　*　　*　　*　　*　　*

Steve woke up with a horribly stiff neck. What in hell was that? Where was he, and what was he doing in the car if that was where he was? It was. Ouch! Ow! Oooo!

Somebody calling?

He thought he'd distinctly heard a woman calling for help. He sat up. Good God, the girl! The Carioca girl.

He leaped out of the car and rushed through the rain to the trailer door. Bolted!

"Hi! Hey! Hey, in there!"

Gloria emerged from a dim but frightful nightmare, in which wild horses were trampling her and people with contracts were screaming for her signature in blood.

"Hello!" she said, weakly.

"Are you all right?"

"What's the matter? Something wrong?"

"Are you all right, I said. Damn it, I'm out in the rain."

"Sure I'm all right. Are you?"

"Yes!" shouted Steve. "Why shouldn't I be? Did I do any yelling? Did I?"

"Did *I?*"

"You did!"

"I didn't."

"You did so!"

There was silence, save for the steady rumble and splash of the rain. Then she heard him going back to the car.

Gloria's head ached. It was so close in here. She got up stiffly and opened a window. Goodness! She quickly closed it to a crack. Honestly, this was impossible. The poor boy must have got soaked. What kind of beastly creatures were women, anyway, to let a man get into such a mess! And all on account of her! Here he'd quite innocently and happily gone off for some fun in the woods all by himself, with his cute gadgets all polished and new and waiting to be played with, and she'd come along and spoiled everything for him—

Gloria began to whimper. I'm a beast, I'm a beast, I'm a nuisance! I hate myself!

She got determinedly up, went to the hook where her coat ought to be—

Oh, that's right. No coat, you incompetent little fool!

She picked up his rain-coat. Still pretty dank, but anyway, she put it on. She had to hold the yard or so of it that would have dragged. She found her shoes, and an old felt hat of Steve's.

Unbolting the door, she went out. Whoo! She hadn't thought it was as bad as this.

Steve was just dozing off again. The rapid hammering on his window made him sit up and bump his head. Dimly, through the foggy window, spattered with big heavy drops, he saw a wild, shouting face.

He pulled down the window with a whirl of the handle. "What's the matter?"

"Are you all right?"

Honestly, this girl must be a lunatic. Good God, that *was* it! Had she escaped from a sanitarium somewhere?

"Go back! You'll get soaked!" he shouted.

"No! I want you to go get dry. I'll stay here."

"Go back! I'm all right. I'm perfectly all right."

"No! Please! Please!"

"I'm all right!" Steve roared. "I swear it! Go back! Go on! Get yourself dry! Good night!"

The wild face disappeared from the window. Steve rolled the window up. Phew! All wet again. Lucky he was immune to colds and all that stuff.

Say, she was a darling. She was an angel! Steve's eyes stared up at the spattered window.

Was it possible that a woman could really be so sweet?

He heard the rain; he listened to the trees. There wasn't any answer from *them*.

X

STEVE woke with the birds. In his eyes the sun was shining; he looked out through the spotted window and saw pale mist rising from the lake, so delicate a blue, so tranquil and gleaming, like satin.

Like the Carioca girl's dress.

Steve crawled out of the car. Oo! For a moment he thought he'd snapped a leg off, but that was just the pain. I'm getting old, that's what. Gee, the sun was going to be hot.

Steve mooned around, wondering what to do. Ordinarily he wouldn't have had any trouble. Your true fisherman, at this early hour, with a good misty lake handy, doesn't stop to wonder about the next step. In his eye is a dreamy look; his lips are set with firm decision, or turned up with pleasant anticipation; his brow is clear; his brain full of lofty thoughts of bucktails, persuaders, smackers, spinners, and wiggle-disks; of fighting bass, of ravenous wall-eyes; of the sharp struggle that cuts the water into spray, the singing line with life at one end and death at the other.

Steve kept on mooning. There was a jay screeching through the giant pines, like a newsboy selling the early morning scandal sheet. A mole had made a little curling hill in the soft earth, twisting round and round, as if he'd done it just to show off. Steve mooned over it.

Wake up, young man! Legions of fishermen are looking down at you and licking their ghostly lips. Will you fail them now? See, there are dark shallow waters under the pines, there are weedy places among the rocks; the eager big-mouths are waiting and flipping their tails with impatience; they have kept themselves in excellent condition; their muscles flex easily, their jaws snap with the fierce joy that only a bass knows. Is there any beauty in the world to compare with theirs? Can a woman snap at a fly or spoon with their grace and precision? Can she cleave the water as they do? Can she shatter it with such a dynamite spring? Can she fight as fiercely, or give such thrilling satisfaction?

Gloria was singing inside the trailer.

Steve listened in a daze, scratching his ears. Suddenly he became aware of the fact that he was in his pajamas, and a particularly villainous pair at that, with green stripes. He ducked back into the car. Whew! Have to get dressed quick. . . .

He reached for his clothes, and then threw them down in disgust. Boiled shirt, black worsted, satin lapels. Bah! A sweet figure he'd cut.

What to do? Far more sensitive than he appeared, Steve was often subject to serious embarrassment over the most trivial things. He couldn't bear to appear ridiculous—in which characteristic, of course, he was not so different from the great mass of males.

He sat in the car, and sulked. Dinner clothes, indeed! Not in a hundred and eighty years.

Young man, the big-mouths don't care about your

clothes. See how superior they are in this, as in every other way! And the small-mouths likewise are indifferent to the proper costuming of the human male, whether for riding, dining, teaing, walking, or just being. The cut of a jacket leaves their blood as cold as it ever was; the tempo of their heart-beats does not quicken at a pink coat or an opera hat, nor do their gills open and shut more rapidly in the society of a pair of pants from Bond Street.

Just about this time the door of the trailer opened and Gloria came out. Steve immediately sat up in the car and looked extremely dignified, as though busy with important thoughts which made it impossible for him to pay any attention to the feeble trivia of everyday.

A gay, smiling face appeared at his window. "Good morning!" Gloria chirped. "Breakfast's ready!"

Steve's dignity was a little bit punctured. "Oh! Good morning," he mumbled. "Did you, ah—did you have a good night?"

"Wonderful! Hurry and come to breakfast."

He smiled at her. "I see you've found some clothes."

"Oh, these?" Gloria looked down at her costume— an old shirt of Steve's, a pair of slacks rolled up about a foot.

"Very becoming," Steve said.

"Thought you'd like 'em," said Gloria.

"Look—would you mind fetching me more of the same? For myself, I mean. I think we know each other well enough so that I needn't appear again in formal costume."

Gloria laughed, and ran in to find him some clothes. Steve looked at the lake. Lake? Lake? Oh, yes, lake. He scrutinized the road, or rather the wreck of it. A river of mud, a wallow in which no car could travel. And over seven miles to Boonsboro, the nearest hamlet!

Well, looked as if she couldn't leave this morning. After all, you had to be reasonable about things, didn't you? Suppose she had got in a jam—it wasn't her fault!

A girl who was as sweet as that—and the first thing in the morning, too—couldn't have done anything to be ashamed of.

And even if she had, who was he to judge? Was he perfect? Nobody had ever told him so—and he had grave doubts himself, sometimes. The important thing about anybody, said Steve, is how he behaves before breakfast. That's the test.

Maybe she's had breakfast, though.

"Have you had breakfast?" he asked as she appeared with his clothes.

"No. Thought I'd wait for you."

See? You could fool him about some things, bonds for instance, but not about women. Hadn't he lived with one for a couple of years? That gave him the right to generalize about the sex, as any man would agree.

"Just wait for me a second and I'll be with you," he said. Gloria disappeared; Steve hustled into slacks and shirt. He entered the trailer, beaming. On the table that had reappeared as the bed disappeared, a steaming pot of coffee, grapefruit juice, and eggs and bacon snapping merrily on the stove.

He felt his face opening like a brook after a cold winter. "Wonderful!"

He sat down opposite her. The trailer was neat; the dishes of last night were all washed and put away. Steve's eyes had the gleam of Columbus, of Balboa, of all the great discoverers, as he looked at her. This gracious being was possibly the supreme specimen of womanhood since the beginning of time. Upon her brow, a diadem. Upon her head, an accolade, with palms.

"Eat your eggs!" Gloria said.

"Oh! Oh certainly. You bet."

No word was spoken for some rich moments. What is better than breakfast in the sweet pine woods in early summer, with every leaf and twig as fresh as on the day of creation—with the storms of the night all over and gone, and the jolly sun starting his long climb? What is better than breakfast under these circumstances and in these surroundings, when somebody else has cooked it? And when she is perhaps the finest example of feminine pulchritude anywhere extant, do your eggs taste better or do they taste worse?

A glassy look was coming into Steve's eyes.

"Don't you feel well this morning?"

What a voice! What a delicious voice!

"Huh?" he said.

"Don't you feel well? You look a bit queer."

"Queer?"

"Well a bit, uh—um—"

"H'm?"

"Don't you hear well?"

"Hear? Oh, certainly, certainly. Yes indeed."

Gloria sighed. A nice boy, but weak somewhere, probably the head. Surly last night, vague today. Wasn't there some mental disease possessing exactly those symptoms? Dementia praecox, wasn't it? The patient is irritable for no apparent reason, and is extremely negativistic to any course of conduct suggested to him. His mood of stubbornness and ill-humor frequently gives way to a prolonged period of lethargy, in which he does not seem to be aware of what is transpiring around him, answers vaguely if at all, and although he eats with good appetite is nevertheless indifferent to his surroundings. This patient—

"H'm," Steve said.

"I beg your pardon?"

"H'm?"

"I thought you said h'm."

"Did you? I mean, did I?"

"Oh, never mind!"

Steve watched her as she got up from the table and went to the door. A goddess, who walked in beauty. Looked damn sweet in his pants. Wonder who she was.

Steve thought he had better make conversation. Obviously she needed to be put at her ease. Charming as she was, he didn't suppose she had had much chance to acquire sophistication and aplomb—after all, *he'd* been all over Europe.

In fact, he'd spent the past two years there, to the woe of his mother, the heavy disapproval of his father, and the almost utter ruin of his business, if you could call it that.

It was clearly up to him to give her the benefit of his wider experience. Not that he intended to deliver any illustrated lectures upon the intriguing, thrilling and fascinating beauties of the Riviera—the idea was, to chat quietly and easily.

He began fooling with a hook-stone. Albert went outside to sniff around. He would do for a look-out. If anybody came, under the bed for Gloria, outside for Steve—and lock the door quick.

"I sharpen up the hooks like this, see? The heads have to be like razors," chatted Steve, holding up some assorted lures for her edification.

"Now this one here, we call it a Doodler, or at least that's the trade name. Pretty neat, isn't it? This is what they call a Smacker. Here we have a drowned mouse, and this one's a swimming mouse. Of course a swimming mouse is much better. Then this is an injured minnow. Swell toward evening, if the water is still. The way it works is this. You take a good easy cast so that this dingus—"

Gloria rattled a cooking pot loudly.

Steve raised his eyebrows. Really, when a gentleman was talking!

Gloria got a mop out of the closet and began slopping it around. "Lift your feet," she said.

"You cast your wiggler or your spp—"

"One side."

"I'll take you fishing and show you."

"Out of the way, please."

"I beg your pardon. Now look at this one here. It's what we call a red-and-white Shannon. Because the color of it is red and white. See? You'd think it ought to be green, wouldn't you, with an Irish name like that? Of course you know what happens when a fish sees red. Or do you? That's the Irish part of it. Fighting Irish. But maybe I can explain it better another way. Do you know much about bull-fights? No? But you do know about *Carmen*, don't you? The opera, *Carmen?*"

"*Carmen? Carmen?*"

"You know—the opera."

"I thought it was a labor union."

"Labor union?"

"You know—street-car conductors." The low pun was really beneath her, she was sure.

"No, it's about a toreador. Really ought to be called a matador, for accuracy, but anyway, you see the bull, when he sees the red, er, scarf or whatever it is the banderillero—"

"Time to wash the dishes—"

"Good! Well, fish are like bulls. Ahh, what snap! What vigor! What coördination! The energy boys, I call 'em. They see that old flicker of red, and they lose their tempers quicker than a movie queen. And whom!"

"Whom! Finish your coffee! And would you mind not talking about fish any more?"

"Oh! Sorry."

Women! Women! Women! They were all alike. No

use. No understanding in 'em. Better get over all your illusions about 'em, and *stay* over 'em.

Suddenly she jumped away from the door and glanced furtively about.

"What's the matter?" he cried.

"Man! Man coming! Hide me—hide me!"

Steve ran to the door and peered out. Why, it was only old Bill Beaselie, the guide he'd hired last night. Bill had beached his skiff down below the trailer, and was walking jauntily up.

"That's just Bill Beaselie, my guide. He's all right."

"No, no, no, no! Quick! Close the door. Go outside! Go outside! Don't let him come in!"

Steve felt a husky push against his back, and out he went. H'mph! Goddess of beauty, huh? She must have bumped off at least six people to be so scared. She must be so notorious that her name was a byword. Pity he'd been in Europe so long. He'd lost touch with American womanhood—in her more public and spectacular manifestations, at least. Scared of old Bill! Steve scowled with vexation.

"Howdy, howdy!" called Bill, coming along with a spry step. "I'm purty late, but had to row across the lake. Road's washed out. Ain't seen a mess like this in twenty years."

"Howdy, Bill! I'll be right with you. I'll just get some tackle from inside the—"

"Say! Didn't git a good look at it last night. She sure is fancy, ain't she? How's she fixed inside?"

"Inside? Oh! Oh, you know. Same as all of them."

"Ain't ever seen the inside of one as fancy as this. Mind if I look her over?"

"Just a minute, Bill. I'll get my tackle and we'll start off. I'll show you around when we come back. Can't waste time now when the bass are breaking water."

"Fresh hatch o' flies got 'em jumping. Nuthin' to that. Man and boy I've caught bass all hours of the day, and I ain't complainin'. Five minutes one way or the other won't—"

"Bill, I want you to take something down to the skiff for me," Steve cut him off.

"Sure, sure."

Steve stared wildly round. Sure, sure, but what? Anguish overcame him. What kind of world was this, anyway? Always getting in a jam over something. No peace. Couldn't even enjoy your breakfast. "Here, Bill, couple of sticks of wood. Take this basket, too, and this monkey wrench."

"Say, what we want all this junk fer?"

"All right, you never mind. I've got a surprise for you."

"Surprise fer me? It ain't my birthday. What we want with this dang old wood? The woods is full of it."

"You wait and see. Make it snappy, Bill, we've got lots on the program."

"Yup, but I can't see what in thunder you want this dang monkey wrench—"

"All right, Bill, I'll show you something you haven't seen before."

"Huh!" Bill muttered to himself, moving off toward

his skiff. "Man and boy I been workin' these here waters for well nigh on sixty years. You can't show me nothin'."

Steve scrambled inside the trailer. "Shhh!" He saw the top of the lounge rise an inch or two. "I'm going off with him. Don't worry! Just got to get my kit. Take it easy, only don't show yourself till we're round the point."

"All right," Gloria whispered.

"Just take it easy. I'll see he doesn't get in here. So long!"

"So long."

Steve went out. Bah! So this was a vacation in the Adirondacks. He met the inquisitive Bill returning.

"Well, guess we better start, Bill."

"All right," Bill gave in. "But doggone it, when you pulled away from the house last evening the old woman asked me to see, first chance I got, if it was a fact that they even got marble bathrooms in these here trailers now—"

"It wouldn't interest you, Bill. I mean, bring the missus out some day." What ailed the man? "Listen, I heard a funny story that'll kill you." (If it only would.) "It seems there was this fellow who was in the chicken business, and he—"

"What feller? Never heard of him."

"This one I'm talking about. So his wife said to him one day, Charlie—"

"Don't know no feller in the chicken business name o' Charlie."

"All right, you're going to know this one extremely well," said Steve grimly. They climbed into the skiff, and Bill shoved off.

"Make for the point, Bill."

"Ain't near so good along there as right up here where we're sot."

"All right, but I've got my heart set on the point. There's a big fellow I'm aiming after. Missed him last year."

"Don't know no big feller over there."

"So this fellow in the chicken business named Charlie . . ."

* * * * * * *

Gloria crawled out. Heavens, that was a close one! Maybe she was a fool to be so careful, but from the experiences she had been through with autograph hounds, she never knew where a fanatic was going to pop up. A fan is bad enough, but a fanatic! They stop at nothing.

This fellow Steve seemed to be about the only person she'd met in ages who didn't recognize her and start reaching for a pen—or her money.

Goodness, she'd entirely forgotten about poor Jim, back home in Hollywood with his new salmon car. She grimaced, and feverishly attacked the breakfast dishes. Were all men mixed up in one way or another with fish?

Steve had the bluest eyes she'd ever seen, but was that any sign? Look at him, off on the lake all day in a boat, with a dull old man for company, hunting for fish!

Well, it would keep him away for awhile, at least. Give her time to find out how her old evil genius was doing with the chase. She bent down beside the radio. Ought to be able to twist the wires together so that she could get reception.

For quite a while she had no luck with the programs. Polish bands, German speeches, Italian singers—and what luck could be worse than that?

She had strong prejudices about music. Of course, you take German singers and Italian bands—they could be pretty awful too. "Ich dich strich stumpfceshreiffpff —putt, oomp, putt, oomp—"

She endured several programs about various products and to a lesser degree about various people in whom she was not in the slightest—

". . . the hunt for the missing star has taken on nation-wide proportions. Federal investigators request that local police coöperate to the full in the rigid search now under way. The confession of Murray Schildecker, eccentric New Jersey truck-driver, that he abducted and murdered the glamorous star, is no longer taken seriously. Murray has been shown to have been home with his mother and invalid sister all during the time that the events that have rocked the nation were transpiring. The movie moguls have doubled their reward. Mr. Moe V. Wurtzberg, agent of the missing star, is reported suffering from a complete nervous breakdown.

Word from her estranged husband in Hollywood has not yet come. . . ."

Gloria smiled coldly. *Dear* Jim!

She snapped the radio off, severed the wires and tucked them out of sight.

"I'm going for a walk," she said to Albert. "And if anybody sees me I guess it's just his hard luck, because *I* don't care."

"Wurr-rurr!" said Albert. He wagged and frisked over her feet. "Ruff!" he said, sniffing at her slacks. Aha! A saunter through the wilds. He'd show the woods he wasn't afraid of 'em!

Gloria hid her things at the back of Steve's wardrobe, gave a hasty look round, and started out. She'd been inside this thing so long it was getting to be hard to tell what she'd do if she were suddenly thrown out into the world. This trailer was worse than college. When you were in college all the deans and teachers and other inmates kept telling you that they were training you to go out in the world and take your place in it—and how did they do it? By shutting you up in boxes and loading you down with rules and forms and procedures and traditions—

Her feelings about college were even stronger than those about music. She'd been to a college in Pittsburgh where they taught you to go crazy in the very quickest time, and according to the very strictest rules. She'd left after the first year, and run away to Paris to study singing. Her poor mother had cabled expostulations and funds—and had praised her ever since, asserting that it had been her own idea all along.

Gloria wandered under the stately trees. Like church, somehow. Grand and solemn. Albert whisked gaily ahead, but not too far ahead. You couldn't scare *him*. She let him lead her deeper into the forest.

*　　*　　*　　*　　*　　*　　*

"Huh!" said Bill Beaselie. "Did you hire me to listen to them dang stories or show you some fish? Four-fifty a day, I git, but that don't come nowhere near what it'll cost you if I have to hear any more of them yarns."

"Slow up, Bill. This place looks good. Under those trees. What do you say?"

"Not near so good as back there where we come from. I know this lake like my own back yard."

"Think I'll try a spook on the first one."

"Frogs is better. You can't beat a frog."

"Bill, you're no purist. Hold her in here."

"Now you take a good frog. Ampytate the legs at the knees so the bass won't be striking too far back. Use a weedless hook—"

"I have a deep aversion to frogs."

"That don't make no odds. Lookee here." Reaching into a gunnysack, he extracted a wriggling peeper and slapped it sharply against the gunwale. It stiffened the frog. Expertly, he cut off the legs and ran a hook through the lips.

"See that there branch hangin' down over the water? You want to toss Mr. Frog right at it and let him plop **into the water.**"

His outfit consisted of an old steel rod that never cost over a dollar, and a reel that was innocent of level winders and anti-backlash devices.

"Lookee now." Bill cast the frog expertly—it dangled just at the proper distance over the quiet water—the frog kicked and dropped off the branch. Instantly something seemed to explode under it—the line whipped free of the tree.

"There's frogs fer yuh!"

"Gee!" said Steve as he netted the bass. "He'll go five pounds."

"Been castin' man and boy fer over seventy years, never seen nothin' to eekal a frog."

"Maybe you're right, but how about a good clean plug, like this one here, for instance? You can't beat a spook."

"Bah! Lucky yer dad can't hear you. He's a great one for frogs, too."

Steve grimaced. He had heard this sermon from Bill many times before. He had to admit, though, that the demonstration was always extremely convincing. It was up to him to show what a purist could do.

"Pull over a trifle," he said. "Hang on." Steve made a long cast, the reel singing. The plug spatted the water. He let it float, then began to reel in, stopped again, vibrated the rod tip.

"What's the matter with me?" Steve asked himself. "Snap all gone."

Maybe it was the fish there was something the matter with.

Something the matter with *bronze-backs?* Legions of departed fishermen lifted ghostly eyebrows at this frightful heresy. *Bronze-backs* leave something to be desired?

The morning wore on. Steve hauled in a fighting six-pounder. Several hours later he hooked a real record-breaker.

"H'mph! Purty fair," old Bill admitted. "What do you say we eat?"

"It's still early. What d'you suppose I came out here for—to get fat? Beautiful morning. Where's the poetry in you, Bill?"

"Mebbe I got poetry in me, but that ain't nothin' agin havin' some fish in me too. You wanted a shore dinner today, didn't you?"

"Of course."

"Takes time to cook it."

"But I'm not hungry, Bill."

"You ain't? It's noon." He cast a shrewd eye at Steve. "Say, what's come over ye? Used to be different kind of feller. You ain't in love, are you?"

"In *what?*"

"Don't git mad. I jist asked the worst thing I could think of, to stiddy you. Them sighs you been fetchin'." He shook his head. "Weak stomach, shouldn't wonder. Take spoonful bakin' soda. Let's eat."

They beached the skiff on a gravelled bank where the big firs marched down close to the water's edge. Steve stretched out comfortably on a bed of pine needles and lazily watched Bill get a fire going and put the coffee and potatoes on to boil. Then he dipped the bass filets in egg batter and rolled them in a pan of flour.

Steve propped his back against a tree. H'm. Something about the simple life, all right. Gave a man a sense of values.

Bill flicked a glance at him.

"What you mumblin' over?"

"Nothing."

"One o' them funny stories o' yourn?"

Steve was drifting off into a warm, dim haze, and forgot to answer. He sighed, and closed his eyes. Wonder what she was doing now. Bathing in the lake? Wonderful creature. Forest sprite. No, forest goddess. It didn't matter. Couldn't let her go now, whatever she had done.

Maybe he could square it for her. Of course he could. He'd never had any experience at squaring things with the police, but there was his father. His father had influence. If—

"Say, wish yer daddy could see you now," Bill broke in on his musing. "It'd make him realize what he's missin', not bein' here."

"No danger. He's too devoted to his work."

"Huh! Devoted, is he? You don't know your pa the way I do. Shouldn't be surprised if he put in an appearance any one o' these days. Knowin' you're up here will sorta work on him."

"I asked him to come along. He wouldn't."

"Askin' ain't the way to git around him. Let him alone for awhile and he'll come, all right. You see."

Steve felt something cold in his chest. Good Lord!

Suppose the old boy did turn up! But he dismissed the thought from his mind, and determined not to let it come back.

"Come an' get it."

He joined Bill over the smoking fish. Good crisp potatoes, canned corn, black coffee. A man couldn't ask for more.

"Ain't nothin' like a couple o' fellers settin' under the trees in the open air, with a good supply o' bass and a pot of coffee," Bill said. "It's the dang old women-folks that stir up trouble. Keep themselves to home, is what I say."

"Oh, I dunno, Bill. Now you take some women, of course you're dead right. But now you take some others—"

"Ain't no others. All women are alike."

"What do you know about women?"

Bill cackled sharply. "What do I know? Man and boy I been watchin' the gals fer sixty-odd years, married one of 'em, got a couple o' datters. What I don't know about women ain't worth that!"

"Bah! You're soured, that's what's the trouble."

"Soured, eh?" Bill snorted. "Young fellers like you don't know nothin'. A purty face and a fair to middlin' ankle will hook you every time."

"Not a chance in the world! I'm cured."

"It's the women that think up the devilment, and the men as does it. I'll bet you my boat that right now there's a lovesick fool of a man somewhere tellin' himself the orneriest gal in town is the sweetest thing on earth, and not bein' able to see that a woman who'll make a fool out of the general run of jackasses won't fool him when his turn comes."

Steve yawned as he sprawled on the warm ground. With his hat over his eyes, he pretended to sleep. It was a pretty spot. Too bad Bill had boiled up like this.

"But it's when they git in trouble and want you to pertect 'em that they git really dangerous," Bill ran on as he scoured his pans with sand. "Soft words! A few tears! And where are you?"

This was getting strangely personal. Steve began to glare into his hat. In a dark deep pool at the foot of a giant rock, a bass broke water with a splash that made him sit up as though he worked on springs.

"Bill, he was as big as a horse! Did you hear him?"

Bill squinted along the water. "Feedin' on frogs," he declared soberly.

"No frogs!" Steve struck a pose. "Shoot if you must this old gray head, but I'll fight it out on this line if it takes all winter! Throw that stuff together, Bill! Come on!"

XI

STEVE wandered back toward the trailer, a little before dusk, dreaming of fish and Gloria, and happy in the thought that he might be able to persuade her to come out with him tomorrow.

But how would he explain her presence to Bill?

He shrank from explaining anything to Bill. Well, postpone the fishing, then. A man couldn't fish all the time.

Maybe they could go swimming together. Give her a bathing suit so that she, er, wouldn't be, um—

He quickened his steps. Wonder how she'd like the record-breaking big-mouth he was bringing home. That ought to fetch her, more than any words from him. There was a delicacy, a subtlety, a dainty persuasive quality about a good fresh bass that beat all the poetry in the world.

That is, around mealtime. Time for poetry after.

He was proud of himself for staying away all day. Tact, that was. Showed her that he wanted her to go right ahead and be at home, feel natural, take it easy. It proved he trusted her too.

Whistling gaily, Steve crossed the point. He could see the trailer now, glistening under the giant trees, and looking for all the world like a home fit for a king.

A king on wheels.

That's me—king on wheels. Why not make a song about that? Come to think of it, he'd been going to tinker with some music on this trip. Lemme see . . .

> *Trailing the sun,*
>   *Trailing the moon,*
> *Hitting the highway*
>   *Midnight and noon—*
> *Go lots of places,*
>   *See everything—*
> *You're—h'm—something on—er—something,*
>   *But on wheels you're a king.*

What was that lyric he'd fooled around with on the way out from New York? Something about wine, women, and—

Oh, yes. How somebody else could take the women, and he would manage all right with wine and song. Steve stopped in his tracks. Hell, did he write that?

Did he ever think that?

Oh, yes, Vivian. All his dreams began to melt, like beautiful palaces of ice cream in the sun. H'm! Reality. He'd forgotten it. The stock market. The upward trend, the feasibility of a somewhat recessive position—

Bah!

Steve went on, muttering to himself. Halfway to the trailer, he pricked up his ears. Then he opened his mouth, and stopped dead.

She was singing one of his songs. Steve had read in books about people's hearts leaping into their throats at great moments in their lives, at crises in their careers so important that from then on they counted the dates from that second onward.

A year and six months from the day I was elected President of the United States. Fifteen weeks after I caught that eight-pounder up on Sand Lake. Things like that.

This was such a crisis. This was such a time.

> *"In such a night as this,*
> *When the sweet wind did gently kiss the trees*
> *And they did make no noise, in such a night*
> *Troilus methinks mounted the Trojan walls . . ."*

Just the same kind of a night. The moon wasn't out, but it would be. The song wasn't "out" either, but it would be by September. At least he hoped so.

He tiptoed up to the trailer door, and stood there in a deep, romantic trance until she had finished. Even he couldn't sing it as well as that.

He waited, until the spell of his own work had lifted itself from him. Then he knocked.

"It's me!" he called. "I've got a surprise for you."

She came to the door, looking very guilty, he thought. Smilingly, he held out the bass. Words could say no more.

"Oh! Oh, take it away!"

"Huh?"

"Take it away! *Quick!*"

"But it's for you—it's my prize catch, I saved it for—"

"I'm sorry, but I thought I made it distinctly clear that I do not wish to have anything to do with any such revolting creatures, ever!"

After she had waited all day long for him to come back, running to peek out of the windows a hundred times, going down to the shore to scan the lake like some simple country girl, and at the utmost risk to herself—what did she get for her pains? A fish!

Thank heavens, Moe wasn't there to laugh at her.

Steve looked as though he might cry. He gazed forlornly down at the beautiful bronze-back dangling from his finger, and turned from her without a word.

Gloria felt her heart sink. She had read about that, too. It was a lot easier to read about it than to feel it. She watched him go dejectedly down to the shore, his shoulders drooping, all the joy blown out of him like the light of a candle in an ill wind.

"Steve!"

No answer. He didn't even pause.

"Steve! Come back."

Goodness, what a baby! She set her mouth in a hard, firm line, and ran after him. This was a crisis in her life too. The blood of countless Newcombes surged in her veins. Not to mention the blood of numerous Rhineharts, Stuarts, Curtises, Williamses, Maddens, Morrisons, MacNeiffs, Potters, Adamses and other families too numerous to mention. All ancestors of hers. All dead, too.

Surging Gloria stopped in back of him. Six feet tall,

and look at him sulking! She smiled, then wiped the smile off.

"I'm sorry. It's a nice fish."

Steve turned round. He looked like a fellow who's lost his mother, his father, his four maiden aunts, and a batch of uncles and cousins.

"I didn't mean to hurt your feelings over it. Let me have it for supper?"

The heroes of many glorious battles, from Crécy to Bull Run, all ancestors of this sublime young woman, rose dimly from their illustrious graves and applauded her with ghostly hands. A halo appeared around her head; and sixty angels wrote her name down in their memory books.

Steve murmured sadly: "I didn't know you really felt that way about fish."

"What nonsense! I'm crazy about fish!"

"Honest?"

"Wild. Absolutely wild."

"Of course I thought anybody *would* go nuts over a chance at a real beauty like this—hauled him out just about noon, and saved him for you."

"Why, that was wonderful of you!"

Steve felt the trance coming back. He tried to speak about the thing that meant so much to him, but somehow he couldn't. Not yet. It was too far beyond any words. But maybe she would sing it again. And one of the new ones too. Gee, how he could compose with a voice like *that* for inspiration! He laughed with joy.

Gloria looked up at him. What simple creatures men

were! A little detail like this was enough to set them up! But about the important things—

They didn't seem to feel the way women did. She sighed. Staying away all day like that!

"I'll fix it for you. I haven't had supper, you know. Came home early in hopes you hadn't either. Of course if you have, why—"

"Oh, no, no, no, no, no. I have coffee and some canned things on the stove."

"Swell! I'll fix the fish for you," Steve said as they stepped back into the trailer. "There's a right way and a wrong way about this business. First, hand me that big pan under there. Then we take Mister Bass, lay him on his side like this, pass the blade gently up round the gills and down the—"

"Excuse me, but do you think it would be all right if I stepped outside for a minute?"

"Huh? Sure, sure!"

Gloria lurched into the air. Steve shrugged his shoulders, and worked happily on.

"Deep fat, smoking hot," he quoted Bill Beaselie. "Egg batter; rub in flour—"

Everything seemed to come along as expected. He dropped the filets in the hot fat and they crackled merrily and turned a golden brown. Imagine sharing this supreme experience with old Bill!

He gazed moonily round. What's all this? He hadn't noticed before. Down the middle of the trailer there was some kind of rope hanging. And over it was slung one of his sheets, gathered up like a portière or something.

"I say, what's the decoration?"

Gloria spoke from out of the hush of the twilight. "That? That's something I saw in the movies. A curtain."

"Oh!"

"I thought since you were a boy scout, and all that, there was no reason why you should get all bent up in the car. Why didn't you tell me you had an extra cot folded away?"

"Modesty." Steve put the fish on a platter.

"I won't violate any of the rules of the troop."

"Thanks."

"It's a nice evening, isn't it?"

What was this? Did he detect a faint note of satire in her voice?

"Dandy. Supper is ready."

Gloria came in, smiling brightly. Her smile was like that of the girl in the adagio dance when her partner is throwing her around; of the has-been actor in the casting office; the salesman in the vice-presidents' chamber; the runner-up in a tennis tournament.

"I'll bet your mouth is watering," said the beaming Steve.

"Oh, yes. Ha, ha."

"Sit down. I'll serve you."

"No, no, no! Let me serve you. Please!"

"Nope. My party. The biggest piece for you. I know you unselfish babies."

"Thanks. Thanks a lot."

"Eat hearty. By the way, I'm glad to see that you're relaxing. I guess it's because there ain't any cops hanging around. You know, I realized all the time you were just fooling me."

"Sure. Just fooling." Something in her tone put a lump in Steve's throat. "I really have no excuse for staying, anyway. I'll leave—"

"Oh, I wasn't suggesting that," Steve hastened to assure her. "I don't want you to go—I mean, at least it's something that can be discussed tomorrow. There's something else I want to say to you. I, ah—" Waves of acute embarrassment suddenly swept over him. He heard his voice become husky. His mouth went dry. What was this? He'd never experienced anything like this before.

Mouthing fish with the gusto—if not the relish—of a sophisticated Eskimo, Gloria trained a pair of strangely liquid eyes on him. "Yes?"

"About your singing."

"Oh. Did you like it?"

An idiot obsession came over Steve. Couldn't show how much his own song had moved him. She'd think him an absolute ass. Mush all through. Make light of it, that was best. Crack a joke, make her laugh.

"Pretty fair for a night-club singer."

"Oh!" Gloria wasn't any too sure about her hackles, but something began to rise in her.

Steve stumbled on. "Of course I wouldn't say you

have a *great* voice, but you have excellent possibilities. The—"

"Thank you!" she said icily. Steve felt the cold work into the marrow of his bones.

"With proper training—" he began again and got no further.

For a moment, Gloria almost told him who she was. Really, this was too much! But she held her tongue.

Well, she was through with the fish, anyway. Miserable, wretched stuff, that only an oaf who couldn't tell a voice when he heard one would bring home.

Still, you know, in a way, it wasn't really so bad. Possibly she had been wrong about bass.

Steve felt his ears getting red. Flunked again. Why didn't they teach you about this sort of thing at Harvard? Instead of all that paleontology and junk like that. Maybe if he tried to gloss things over a bit she would loosen up and be herself again. Difficult, this girl.

"Would you like me to take you to Boonsboro tonight in the car? You could hide out there until the—er—the police are through looking for you."

"That's nice of you, but I suspect you just want to be rid of me."

One of the things women do, Steve said to himself, is to try to put *you* in the wrong when they don't feel so comfortable in it themselves.

"Of course," he reminded her gently, "I never invited you on this trip in the first place."

"Oh! I see! Very well, I won't bother you a minute longer."

Hell, he'd certainly sunk himself now. That's the way women were—first they did some damn thing, then they sulked over it, then they got you mad, then they made you say something you never would have dreamed of, and then they jumped on you.

"Listen, I didn't mean that I *regretted* having you here, but I was just reminding you that you have no ground for reproaches—yet."

Gloria fussed back and forth, getting her clothes out. There weren't many. She didn't speak. How could she? There was nothing to say on her side, at least nothing she could think of. She'd made a mess of everything, and spoiled this nice boy's fun. She'd clear out. Why make him pay for her troubles any longer? Of course another thing women do is to act very cool and hard when they're feeling terribly sentimental and soft. What would happen to them if they let their feelings show? Gloria strode around, bumping into things. The noise helped to keep her mind off what lay ahead.

"Look here, Miss Glamorous, I can't help it if you're beautiful."

Gloria didn't say anything.

"I guess maybe you don't like me. But that's not the point. What I'm interested in right now is helping you out of your trouble, not in an exchange of compliments. So just take it easy while we figure out what to do. Sit down!"

"What?" said Gloria.

"Sit down!"

"I won't!"

"What would your mama say if she saw you acting like such a baby? H'm? She'd call you a naughty girl and make you go stand in the corner."

"I don't care."

"Come on, little girl. Sit down and be good."

Gloria was melting softly away. What a darling he was! He could be so strong and stern. And then so persuasive. If she once let him see what was happening to her, there would be no more simple life, no more anything but flight. She looked as cool as she could, which isn't very cool when you have such lips and eyes as hers. She sat down.

"That's fine. Now, look. Suppose I take you into town tonight and we find you a good quiet place to put yourself up. Tourist home or something. We'll figure out a name and a complete history for you. Then, when the trouble blows over, I'll just sneak you off wherever you want to go and—"

He could be kind and generous, thought Gloria. With a touch of panic, she realized she wanted to kiss him. She looked firmly out of the window. Then she stared at her shoes. The conversation lagged badly.

"You needn't look so distressed. You'll be free of my society in a few hours, and you can forget all about it."

Gloria didn't answer. His humility touched her. She wanted to hug him, but she stared resolutely up at the ceiling.

"You scared of being recognized?"

She jumped. "What?"

"I thought so. Afraid somebody'll know who you are?"

"Why should I be? I'm just a—a night-club girl."

"Sure, sure, but *such* a night-club girl!"

Gloomy silence fell. Steve fiddled with his hook-stone again. Should he entertain her some more about the delicate intricacies of casting? No, better not. She seemed to have some peculiar antipathy to the subject. What a girl!

There was a poem Mark Twain quoted once. He'd forgotten just what the occasion was, but it seemed to him that the old boy had been called upon to propose a toast to the ladies at some dinner. And he'd started off on an elaborate introduction to the poem he was going to quote. Said it was perhaps the noblest and most moving tribute to the sex ever conceived. Said it epitomized all their sweet and wonderful qualities. Said it just summed up everything. Along comes the poem.

"Woman!" says old Mark, and pauses.

> *"Woman! Woman, er—*
> *Woman."*

There is wild applause. Second verse.

> *"Alas! Alas. Er—*
> *Alas, alas, alas."*

That's all Mark could remember of the poem, but anyway, there it was, and so beautiful and touching, too.

Gloria spoke at last.

"I appreciate everything you say, but you see if I go to some town I'll be stranded. Does it have a railroad?"

"No."

"And I'll be all alone. I'll be a stranger. And people will begin to wonder about me, and ask questions."

"Tell 'em the Carioca story."

"It's not good enough for them."

"*I* liked it."

"Thanks."

"Well," he decided, "stay here if you like. It's up to you." He was beginning to feel very ill at ease. He coughed, and got up. "I, ah—I think I'll take a little stroll down the lake. There's a moon. Like to come along?"

"No, thanks."

"I'll look after you."

"I'd love to go, but really I think I'd better stay here," she said in a frigid voice.

"Oh! Sorry to suggest anything so unwelcome. Good night," he growled, stumbling over the threshold. The door closed after him with a bang.

Wandering off in the pale light of the moon, he sighed heavily. Blankly he gazed up into the sky; stared down at his feet; looked all around and shook his head. The gentle air of evening laid a kiss against his cheek; the moonbeams gilded his brow. It wasn't indigestion. What could be wrong with the world?

*　　*　　*　　*　　*　　*　　*

"Should I tell him? Should I just tell him who I am and have all this hypocrisy over with?"

Gloria brooded to herself, staring up at the ceiling with a fixed, rapt look.

"Yes, and then he'll know I'm married, and rich, and—"

Why shouldn't he know all that? H'm? Speak up, Miss Newcombe.

"Oh, I don't know. Just because."

Because! Look here, if you women would ever stop being childish and try to face the difficulties you bring upon yourselves and others, maybe you'd make this a happier world.

"Would we?"

Yes, you would.

Gloria got up and stamped her foot. "I'm leaving!" she snapped—and sat down, and began to dab at her eyes.

* * * * * * *

Perched on a log, his pipe cold in his teeth, Steve scowled at the waters of Sand Lake, rippling in the moonlight.

"Sure, and if I tell her about myself, then what? I've got a wife, haven't I? If you could call it that. Guess she won't be a wife much longer. At the same time, what right have I to lead a lovely, beautiful girl to suppose that I—"

Who's leading her, you sap?

"Well, I mean if I had a chance."

Hah! That's it, is it?

"Sure. A man's got to speak up, or some other fellow will."

And what piece do you propose to speak, Mr. Romanticist-in-the-Moonlight?

"A good slick piece, that's what. Tell her that I— that she—"

Go on. Don't stammer.

"That we—that maybe if things got straightened out for me, and she was agreeable, why then that she, that I might be agreeable to—"

Leave out a few pronouns and get down to business.

"I love her. Good gravy! I'm wild about her. I think she's the most beautiful girl in the world. Needs a little training, and she'll be perfect. Teach her to sing, too. Maybe write a song for her. I'll—"

*   *   *   *   *   *   *

"Hello!" he greeted her ten minutes later. "I came back."

"I see you did!"

Now that he could reach out and touch her, he was left without words. He couldn't understand this self-consciousness. Awkwardly he edged over to the piano. "Would you like a little music?"

"Just love it."

"I really liked your singing—a lot." (The way you'd say, "I liked those dill pickles you brought home from the grocery store—very much.")

Damn it, he couldn't say it in words. Maybe he could tell her in music. He closed his eyes and let his hands wander over the keys . . . never mind his own junk now. Chopin, that romantic one they always play in the love scenes at the movies. . . . He caressed the notes, and gave them all the delicate shading his skill could evoke . . . then Beethoven, the good old *Moonlight Sonata.*

She stood beside him. "Let me be the first to congratulate you. Your work is as great as that of—shall we say—two composers? I'm sure they won't mind."

Steve laughed. "That's sweet of you. But you don't want to hear my tripe. Listen to old Ludwig, lonely old Ludwig, who couldn't hear. . . ."

Gloria stood perfectly still, while the legato—liquid, singing and full of pain distilled into a form so pure that nothing earthly remained—filled the warm night and transfigured it. She saw a thin little moon just rising over the lake, in a sky of frozen silver.

Could she have been wrong about men? Was it just possible that something she had always hoped for in a man, and never believed in, was really there after all?

She remembered similar evenings with poor old Jim, when she'd tried so hard to make herself believe that they were happily married and that there was a common bond between them. That must have been a long time ago—or maybe it just seemed long. The only music Jim seemed to care about was the roar from one of his motors—the only poetry he had in him was his mystical rapture over a certain highly specialized kind of engraving upon bank paper.

Gloria sighed, and looked at Steve's hands on the

piano keys. So delicate in their touch, and yet as strong as iron. So—

"What's the matter?" he asked, smiling at her. "Lonesome?"

"Oh! Oh, no, no!" she assured him heartily. "It's just so—quiet—and peaceful—and—and different here—"

Steve nodded. He knew what she meant. He felt that way too. This was the first time he had been able to relax with a woman around for—well, for as long as he cared to remember. When memory went back too far, it recalled Vivian and her caustic toleration of his moods and his music. You wouldn't think toleration could be caustic—but hers could.

Steve sighed too. "Swell here," he murmured. He puffed his pipe dreamily. "Dulls the edges of one's mistakes—doesn't it?"

"Humph?" Gloria inquired inelegantly.

"I said it dulls the edges of one's mistakes—puts you definitely on the alkaline side," said Steve.

"Doesn't it," she sighed.

*   *   *   *   *   *   *

"Mind telling me who you really are?" he asked after a long silence.

"What does it matter? Who should I be, anyway? Minnie Rumpelmayer?"

"I have the funny feeling that I've seen you somewhere.

"Oh."

"There's something about your face."

"Thank you. Do I have a kind face?"

"It doesn't have to be kind."

"My dear Mr. Greene, that is high praise. By the way, would you mind telling me where we are? I never asked."

"Where we are? Oh!" Steve came out of his trance. "We're at Sand Lake. Why?"

Gloria jumped. Sand Lake? Sand Lake? Where had she heard it mentioned—and very recently?

"Would you sing a song of mine?" Steve asked after another long silence. "I've got something here that's never been sung."

"Sure. If you'll show me how."

"You bet, glad to."

"It isn't often I get a chance for any coaching, you see."

This was lost on Steve. He hunted through his scores. *Trio for flute, violin and pianoforte . . . Lament for a lonesome harpsichord . . . Quartet in A Major, unfinished . . .* relics of his first yearnings to be another Mozart. He'd given that up after a while and tried just to be himself. That was hard, too.

"You know it's awfully hard just to be yourself?" he said, turning to her.

"I've noticed it." (Sand Lake! Now *who* had said something about this very place?)

"Anything a little fresh, a little strange—people don't expect that, so they hate it. They called Beethoven a barbarian, an ignoramus and a musical boor. They said Brahms marked the decline of German music—

no good. If they do that to the big fellows, what do they do to the little ones like me?"

"What *do* they do?"

"They don't do anything at all. They won't even listen. So do you know what I'm going to do?"

"What are you going to do?"

"I'm going to write a few songs that are just standard oatmeal stuff, with a hint of something different in them, but not enough to scare anybody. Then when I get that far I'll cut down on the oatmeal and increase the dose of the something different, until finally I throw all the oatmeal away and have nothing but—"

"But what?"

"Whatever it is I've got. And then I can do some serious work and get it listened to. See? A couple of concertos, things like that."

"Let me try this song. It looks as though it had very little oatmeal in it."

"That one? H'm. I'll serve it to you for breakfast. But still, maybe you'd like it. I'll play it over anyway."

"By the way, what's all this about women?"

"Women?"

"I came across some notes—let's see. Here they are."

"Oh, those," Steve said, looking rather guiltily at a handful of scores and jottings. *You take wine, I'll take . . . Woman, stay 'way from my door . . . Ring-around, fling-around, cling-around . . .*

"You don't seem to like us very much. Why?"

"Sure I like you. Crazy about you."

"You must have been terribly disappointed in some

girl, and it hurt you so much that you tried to believe that all of us were the same."

"Do you think so?"

"It's the oldest and feeblest lie in the world."

"Some of you are nice."

"That's high praise, from you."

"You bet it is. Look, I've been mulling something around the last couple of days—the tune isn't hammered out just right and the words aren't all there, either. And it's another breakfast song—but this is how it goes—"

He sketched out the melody, revising a note or two as he went along.

"Like the tune?"

Gloria nodded.

"Here are some words for you." He tossed her a slip of paper. "All right?"

"What's this *something* and *something* part?"

"That's you. *She's got something and something, and she's got something more . . .*"

"Go on and play."

"Okay."

Gloria sang the words lightly:

> *"Trailing the sun,*
> *Trailing the moon,*
> *Hitting the highway*
> *Midnight and noon—*
> *Go lots of places,*
> *See everything—*

Here's where the somethings come."

Steve sang:

"You're a slave in the traces—"

Gloria finished:

"But on wheels you're a king!"

He applauded her loudly. She applauded him. They both took bows.

"Just a minute, Mr. Composer, was that clapping for the song or for the singer?"

"That's what I was going to ask you."

"Well, I'll tell you what we can do," said Gloria. "I'll applaud my singing and you applaud your composing—and we'll both be happy!"

"It's a bargain, lady."

It was a happy beginning. The little thin moon rose high in the sky: their voices rose, too, astonishing Albert and the quiet trees.

*   *   *   *   *   *   *

"Well, guess it's bedtime."

It was almost midnight.

"You can make yourself comfy with blankets and pillows—there seems to be an abundance of them—and have one end of the trailer to yourself," Gloria informed him. "I'll have the other end. That ought to satisfy everybody—even you."

"H'm! Very tricky." Steve yanked at the curtain. It almost collapsed.

"Hi! Be careful!"

"Sorry. Just testing it."

"Why do you have to test it?"

"We eagle scouts always do. One of our rules."

*   *   *   *   *   *   *

Steve awoke from a peaceful slumber, some time later, to the sound of gnawing and growling. He rubbed his eyes and stared at the dim folds of the curtain. It was shaking violently.

"What's this? Does she have epilepsy?" he muttered.

Then he saw one of Albert's paws. Oh, Albert!

Steve lay and watched that paw. It was busy with the curtain. So were Albert's teeth—shaking it like a rat.

What would an eagle scout do under these circumstances? Obviously he would not hesitate a second. Leaping quietly out of bed, he would remonstrate with the recalcitrant canine, also quietly, and if remonstration failed to accomplish the desired effect, he would engage the canine's attention with a few well-chosen rope tricks, knots, loops, etc., until he was completely fascinated by them and desired to enter the troop himself. Should the canine's attention wander at any time to the curtain, our eagle scout would win it back by a few wise, firm words, possibly an amusing story or two, or perhaps a saucer of milk.

Steve lay still. Albert wrestled with the cord that fastened the curtain.

An eagle scout would wrestle with Albert.

"Wurr-uff!" said Albert suddenly. The curtain plopped down over him and muffled his cry of victory.

Gloria sat up in terror, clutching the bedclothes.

"What's the matter? Who is it? Oh!"

Steve pretended to be asleep.

"What do you mean by scaring me like that?" She really did sound frightened.

There was silence, except for the subdued growling of Albert and the weird cry of a loon from across the lake.

"Please put it back up."

Steve did an elaborate imitation of a man waking out of a profound slumber.

"Hi!" he said. "Who's there?"

"I think that was a mean trick. After all the trouble I went to—"

"Go to sleep."

"I can't go to sleep. My heart is beating like a trip-hammer."

Steve got up and fumbled around with the curtain. How did this damn thing work, anyway? The loon laughed madly from across the lake.

"I'm afraid it's busted," he grumbled. "But don't worry, I'll go out and get some logs and build a wall. Just a minute till I get a hammer and some nails. Where's my saw? Where'd you put my saw?"

"I never saw your old saw."

Steve suddenly got a brilliant idea. Clutching the table-top, he pulled it over and set it down on its edge between them. It wasn't much more than waist high, but still, it was a barrier.

"There you are!" he said. "Now we're both safe."

"You think you're bright, don't you?"

"They all say I am. Good night, Miss Girl Scout."

"Good night. And if you come beyond that wall I'll shoot."

"If I get that far you'll have to shoot."

XII

TRUDGING dutifully off to meet Bill the next morning, Steve bore his rod, not like a proud lance, but like some old worn-out broomstick. His head buzzed; his eyes blinked strangely; his feet dragged along.

Bill was waiting for him at the point.

"Say! Thought you was never comin'! Was jest headin' up fer your trailer. Fishin' ought to be good today."

Steve stumbled into the skiff. Ah, to be in a gondola, under the moon!

Bill shoved off, gabbling noisily. Steve heard his voice as from a great distance. Aeons of time seemed to pass, as if he were one of those hasheesh smokers who under the influence of their drug are conscious of infinity in the space of a few seconds. Bill was pretty impatient with him. Here he'd thought old Ev Greene's boy was a likely lad, who with proper supervision might develop into a respectable fisherman and hence into a possessor of all manly virtues—and look at him mooning there!

"Lookit here, Steve, that ain't proper castin'. I'm surprised at a feller with your college trainin'."

"H'm? What did you say, Bill?"

"Lookit here, my boy, I'm gettin' four-fifty a day fer showin' you some fish, not lullin' you to sleep."

"Sure, sure. That's certainly so, Bill. Ha, ha."

Neither fisherman had noticed the quiet approach of two state troopers through the woods. The officers looked long and earnestly at them, and continued on. Then one of them spoke to the other, and they turned back.

"Who you got there, Bill?"

Bill scowled. Likely spot, in there among the lily pads—no good now.

"Name's Mister Greene! Steve Greene of New York. I've known his daddy, man and boy, these forty year. Somethin' wrong?"

"That's my trailer parked up there beyond the point," Steve explained.

"Oh—" The troopers started to trudge away.

"Say, what's goin' on?" Bill Beaselie yelled. "Who you lookin' fer?"

"Where you been, Bill? Thought you got around."

"You never mind where I been. What's up?"

"Trouble. Looking for a couple of mugs from New York. Bank hold-up."

"Say! That right?"

"Hiding out around here somewhere. We're hunting for their girl friend."

"Sounds like a regular romance," said Steve. "Who is she?"

"Girl from the Carioca Club. Know anything about it?"

"The what?"

"Night club in New York. They used her car for

the job. We got a tip she'll meet him up here. Seen anybody around?"

Steve felt a chill go through his bones. Then he got hot all over.

"Not a soul."

"Okay." The troopers stalked off.

Bill sighed heavily. "Say, this here country'll be hoppin'! Nothin' like this ever hit these here woods before, except when them gangsters was up at Hull's Landing."

Steve didn't answer.

"Hi! Don't let her drift in too far!"

Steve cast in a trance. With ten per cent of his skill and less than that of his patience, he went through the motions of tempting the wary bass and pike which. should be waiting behind these stumps, or under these promising pads. Nothing but trouble seemed to happen—he fouled his line, developed a series of backlashes, lost his patience. He was trying to keep a certain person out of his mind by means of every device he knew. He counted; he whistled; he told Bill some more stories; he concentrated upon the beauties and the qualities of *micropterus salmoides, micropterus dolomieu,* and *stizostedion vitreum.* It didn't work at all. He was so shaken that he couldn't concentrate on anything.

Could it be his girl they were after? Impossible! That didn't fit her story at all. Her story? She hadn't told any—just made a few cracks about singing in the Carioca Club, and acted scared. But she hadn't been acting when she was scared!

Here he'd sheltered her and fed her and looked after her and hidden her, and she didn't trust him any more than to tell him a fool story like that!

Was it a fool story? She was obviously some kind of a singer, and she was obviously in trouble, just as she had said.

"Don't you think they were just stringing us along, Bill?"

"How do you mean, Steve?"

"About that bank hold-up stuff. Sounds silly. And that night-club girl!"

"Search me. I dunno. Say, ain't you got a radio in that trailer? Mebbe some news comin' in."

"Something gone wrong with my set. But why on earth would they be on the radio?" He sounded guileless enough.

"Well, I dunno. I jest thought of it. Mebbe we better git over to Clint Hodgkins' place. He's got a set."

"Listen, Bill, for an old-timer you get more worked up than anybody I ever saw. Just relax. Take it in your stride."

"Oh, I ain't worked up none. But we ain't had no real excitement here in years. I kinda hate to miss anythin'—"

"How about fishing?"

"Seems to me the wind ain't right fer fishin'."

Steve concealed his relief as well as he could.

"All right, Bill, you go on over to Hodgkins' and enjoy yourself. I'm going back to putter round the car. You can put me ashore here."

Bill was willing enough. His sharp eyes were combing the bank. Them troopers wouldn't be far away. Git them to loosen up a bit, shouldn't wonder. Talk to 'em right. They knew there wasn't a feller in the whole country that knew the lay of the land half as well as old Bill Beaselie.

He said: "See you in the morning," as Steve stepped out of the skiff.

*　　*　　*　　*　　*　　*　　*

Gloria and Albert had found a perfect spot. Deep in the woods, in a little hollow, there was a waterfall and a pool. It was really Albert who found it. He hadn't walked very far this morning before something atavistic stirred within him; and forgetting all about the terrifying noises of the night, and the more terrifying creatures that made the noises, he had darted off on a fascinating trail.

Gloria called, and then she followed. Slanting bands of light came through the thick boughs and spangled the soft brown carpet of needles. It was easy enough to make one's way among the trees, for brush didn't grow very far under their somber shade. Once in a while there would be a little clearing, and here a clutter of vivid green leaves and eager branches reaching toward the light would interrupt her progress.

She stopped suddenly; Albert stopped too. There ahead of them, deep in the shade, stood a delicate fawn, its huge eyes looking straight at them. It had been drinking from a pool. Another moment, and it was gone; she saw its white tail flash among the trees.

Albert was hysterical. The echoes rang with his doughty voice.

"Albert! Hush! You'll scare everything within a mile."

Gloria ran to the pool and bent down to look at herself in the water. It was so still and clear—and all around were the fine quiet trees. You couldn't see out in any direction.

She had been wanting a swim ever since she awoke. The white fall, like a frothing cascade of milk, was too much for her. It made her think of Cleopatra—she bathed in milk, didn't she? Well, here was some water. Nothing more logical than that.

For sheer joy in the pool and the trees, and in being so lucky as to find them, Gloria began to sing.

She'd come here every morning. This was perfect. After all, Hollywood had lots of pools, but what were they made of? Cement and tile. Here was moss, and look at those rocks, looking just as natural! In fact, they *were* natural. What a relief from pictures! No Kleig lights, no sound track, no nagging directors— no contracts.

She tossed Steve's shirt and slacks on the bank, and dipped her feet in the pool. O-ooo!

Still, it was nice when it was cold, after you got over the first shock. This Hollywood life had softened her. What would her mother say? Hadn't she trained her not to be afraid of cold water?

Singing bravely, Gloria slipped down into the glassy pool. Once she had got the first of it over with, it would be wonderful. She let the water come over her head, shook it smartly, and came up laughing.

Albert's eyes watched her from the bank. They began to look a little sad. This selfish passion for wetness! He'd fought it for years in her, and no results. No thanks, even. He didn't expect human beings to learn about the best things of life all at once—for although they had a certain rudimentary kind of intelligence, which sometimes even approached a point where it was almost doglike, still it always left something to be desired.

*   *   *   *   *   *   *

Inside Steve's trailer, two earnest young state troopers looked at each other dubiously.

"Well, it only goes to show you never can tell about these clean-cut birds," said one.

"Didn't I say he sounded funny?" said the other.

"Yeah, but Bill claims he's all right."

"H'm. Nothing said about having his wife with him, was there?" The earnest young officer held up various samples of Gloria's clothing.

"Naw, but you can't say anything till you're sure."

"Would I put my foot in my mouth?"

"Suit me if you did. It'd probably be a good fit."

"Why on earth did you make up that fool story about a couple of gangsters—and a girl from the Carioca Club?"

"Oh, I dunno. Thought it would put him off-guard."

"But why the Carioca Club?"

"Well, I picked that off the radio—it's a joint in the

building where Gloria Newcombe was seen last. It just popped into my head."

"Shh! Here he comes."

They peered out at Steve, hurrying along under the trees toward the trailer.

"Looks worried, if you ask me."

"Well, if he's *got* a wife, isn't that plenty good reason?"

"Pipe down, I tell you. I'll handle him."

Steve came whistling along; but it was one of those weak, anxious whistles, the kind men emit when things are going wrong.

"Hello!" he called, when he was a few steps away. His voice was like the gentle cooing of a dove. The troopers looked at each other. Then he entered.

"Hi! What's up?" he said.

Silently, Corporal Thurber, the more earnest of the two troopers, held a pair of silk step-ins up to Steve. "These yours?"

The other trooper stifled a sudden guffaw.

"What nice things you've got in your wardrobe," continued Corporal Thurber, in a tone of ponderous reproach. "You married?"

Steve looked him coldly in the eye. "Yup," he said.

"Where's the missus?"

"The what?"

"I said, where's the missus?"

"Oh. I thought that was what you said. Why, she's in—ah—Southampton."

"Oh, she is, huh?"

"Where would she be, up here?" Steve asked belligerently. "You think I'd be fool enough to cart a woman along on a fishing trip? What kind of a vacation would that be for a man?"

There was one thing Steve had learned from his wife —when in a weak position, act very, very strong. Be domineering, be accusing, put the other fellow on the spot, make him feel silly, attack his views on religion, politics, the weather, the home, mother, the flag—on anything you possibly can find. This technique, in Vivian's hands, had reduced *him* to a helpless muddle many a time. He scowled grimly at the officers.

"Now you boys look here. I'm willing to play along with you if you just act like civilized human beings. But when you start fumbling around with my wife's— ah—property on some ridiculous pretext—"

"That's all right, Doc. Just keep your shirt on. We're only doing our duty."

"Here a guy comes up to the Adirondacks for a quiet, peaceful fishing trip when he's already on the edge of a nervous breakdown, and what does he find? A bunch of gangsters running around in the woods, wild women hiding out in the swamps, cops popping out at him from inside his own trailer—damn it, I've got a good mind to pack up and go back to New York."

"Take it easy, take it easy."

"You've got Bill Beaselie so wrought up he can't do a lick of fishing today. Is that fair?"

"You know," said the more earnest of the troopers, "you're just one of these cases of jitters you get in the cities. You better just relax. Next time your wife leaves some of her things in your trailer you better put 'em away where they belong. Come on, Hank. Let's be going.''

The officers clumped out. Steve exhaled, and slumped down on the piano bench. Just for atmosphere, he played a few bars of his most anti-feminist compositions, until they were out of sight.

Then he leaped for the door. What next? What next? And what would he do about all this? He was getting in a terrible spot. He set off anxiously into the woods. Where could she be? If only he could rush off in all directions at once! He started to call, and then stopped. That would be the worst thing he could do.

*   *   *   *   *   *   *

Gloria was enjoying herself so utterly that it seemed impossible for such pleasure to last. She splashed the water into a shower, and laughed with joy.

Albert suddenly agitated his nostrils and pricked up his ears. Ah! Somebody coming. Albert smiled to himself. Liked to be wet, huh? If their host, now standing on the bank and staring at her, had anything to say about it, Albert guessed there would be a serious objection. Human beings couldn't *all* approve of her goings-on.

Gloria shrieked. Steve started back.

"What do you mean coming here like this? Can't you see I'm bathing?" she cried, retreating into deeper water.

Steve was wordless. He just made gestures.

"Go away! Go away and leave me at once, or I'll scream!"

"Hold on, don't get mad," he sputtered helplessly. "I was looking for you."

"I should say you were!"

"I only wanted to tell you some bad news," he said.

"Go away!"

"The state troopers are looking for a girl, and I shouldn't be surprised if it's you. In fact, I don't see who else she could possibly be."

"Oh!"

"Better get back to the trailer in a hurry."

"How *can* I?"

"I'll beat it. For goodness' sake, don't be so coy. *I* wouldn't look at you."

"Oh, indeed!"

"The troopers found some of your clothes in the trailer. If you want my advice, you'll stow this modesty stuff, slip into some clothes and get to cover in a hurry." With which sound advice, Steve departed. But he loitered along the way, expecting her to catch up. More and more slowly he went, but no Carioca girl.

Carioca? Oh, hell! It was all too much for him. He finally reached the trailer and went inside. Let's see. Where could she hide? The bathroom? No. Bill was interested in the bathroom. The folding bed? That was it. Close quarters, but she'd be safe there.

But suppose she really was mixed up in this mess? Nonsense! She *couldn't* be. Or if she was, somebody had tricked her into it. One thing certain, he was going to stand by her, whatever happened.

But she couldn't be a criminal! No? Why couldn't she? Why was she so scared? Think of Milady de Winter! Think of Messalina!

He peered anxiously among the trees. She was nowhere in sight. He began to feel slightly sick.

Then he saw her. She was sitting on a fallen log, with her face in her hands.

He ran up to her. "What's the matter? Are you hurt?"

Gloria lifted a miserable face. "Everything's the matter. I only wanted to get away from something unpleasant. I didn't expect the police to track me down like this. Now I've involved you—and I'm so sorry! You've really been so good about it—"

"Nonsense! he exclaimed. "Don't you worry about me. I want to help you. Really I do."

"But kidnapping—"

Steve stared at her blankly.

"Who said anything about kidnapping? The troopers didn't say—"

"But that's really why they're looking for me," Gloria insisted. She was connecting the police with those radio broadcasts, and completely forgetting her Carioca Club story.

Steve just stood and stared at her. This case appeared to have complications that went deeper than he had imagined. But it didn't matter, he told himself. Somehow, it was all a ghastly, hideous mistake. Was there anything criminal in the long curve of those lips? in the depths of those eyes? Hardly!

"I *must* get away from here," Gloria sighed. "It might be very unpleasant for you if they found me—"

"No, no! You can't go!" said Steve. "You wouldn't have a chance. I knew it must be you they wanted, but it—it took me back a little to have you admit it. But I don't care what the charge is against you, they're not going to pick you up if I can help it."

"Charge—!" Gloria gasped.

"Well, charge—or whatever you call it—"

"Oh—do you mean that Carioca Club business?" she asked, light breaking on her at last.

"Don't tell me there's something else," he exclaimed.

Gloria began to feel easier. So he really believed that absurd Caricoa Club story after all. But here he stood, believing her a fugitive from justice, yet ready to protect her with his life, limb and trailer. Surely that was something. It did things to Gloria.

"Why are you so kind to me?" she asked, her voice doing tricks. "You're so generous—"

"Generous, hell! I'm an ass and a fool and all the rest of it. That's why I'm helping you. If I didn't know better I might even think I was falling in love with you. But you can forget that. You got yourself into a mess, and there's nothing I can do now but get you out of it. . . . Stand up!" he barked. "You're going back to the trailer this minute and lie low for a day or two."

He grabbed her roughly by the arm and hurried her along.

Gloria went without protest. This brute striding along beside her had the strength of seven devils in his long fingers. But it was delightful, de—— What was it he had said about love? Anyway, he had advised her to forget it. Naturally, he didn't mean that. Something might be done about—

Her train of thought piled up in sharp and hopeless collision. There was Jim. She had quite forgotten about Jim and his mechanical toys.

Steve felt her shiver.

"Stayed in the water too long," he said.

"Mmmm—" she agreed.

XIII

DOWN at the edge of the lake, a clump of bushes rustled and shook.

"Come on out of there," said Corporal Thurber.

Bill Beaselie popped out of hiding. "What's up?" he piped.

"Shh! Take it easy," said Corporal Thurber. "I think he's got her with him."

Bill Beaselie's eyes grew as round as a cat's. "Ha! I knowed it the minute I seen him that first night. Looked mighty funny, all them curtains closed. My old woman she says to me, 'Bill Beaselie,' she says, 'no man acts shifty-eyed and oneasy without a woman in it somewhere.' You can't fool my old wo—"

"Sure, sure, *we* wouldn't try to, Bill. And don't you try, yourself. Now listen. He thinks he's fooled *us*, see? So he's probably gone off to get the girl, and then he'll be clearing out. Now Bill, you're guiding this man, but your duty is to help us—and maybe help him, too. Chances are he doesn't know what she's letting him in for. What do you say?"

Bill rubbed his chin thoughtfully. "Well," he said at last, "duty is duty. What ye want me to do?"

"Listen—" said the corporal.

*　　*　　*　　*　　*　　*　　*

179

Back in the trailer, Steve and Gloria sat staring gloomily at the floor. There was so much between them that couldn't seem to get itself said. Gloria was thinking of what she would have to go back to—Steve was wondering what it was.

"Cheer up," he said gently. "We don't care about a few cops. Let's figure out something. Maybe I could run you over the line into Canada—"

Gloria lifted her head and looked into his eyes. They were still the bluest she had ever seen—and full of goodness and gentleness. It was almost too much for her.

Steve found himself gazing at her from across the table. All his brave words melted away; he felt his heart beating faster. "You—you've got to be brave about this," he stammered. Impulsively, he flung out a protecting hand.

In his excitement his elbow knocked over the pitcher of canned milk. Albert wagged his tail and leaped forward, his tongue out toward the trickling stream.

At this moment Bill Beaselie, treading as softly as a cat, edged his face inside the door of the trailer in order to see what he could see.

He took a good long look, edged his face out again, and disappeared in the woods.

Distracted by Albert and the pounding of her heart, Gloria tried to break the spell by stooping down and pretending to scold the dog.

"Albert! All over my nice clean floor!" she cried.

Cursing Fate, his elbow, the milk pitcher and the dog (silently of course) Steve picked up the pitcher. "Look here," he said sternly. "There's something I've been wanting to ask you."

"Just a minute, till I get the mop."

"Never mind the mop. Albert will take care of that department all right."

Gloria's head was whirling; his voice seemed a long way off. She looked up at him again.

The sound of off-key whistling came to their ears— they jumped apart. "Oh, Lord! Lift up the couch!" Gloria ran for her hiding-place.

Steve fumbled at the catch. "Quick! Don't let them see you!" he whispered. Pushing her out of sight, he flopped down on the cushions just in time.

Bill Beaselie, pretending a great innocence, ambled up to the trailer door. This time he was carrying his oars, which he leaned carefully against the trailer. As for the oar locks, he tossed them carefully underneath the car. Then he knocked. "Hi there, Steve! Bein' over on this side of the lake, thought I'd drop in," he piped, sticking his head inside.

Steve swallowed hard. His voice came in a croak. "Hello, Bill! Come right in. Always glad to see you. Hear anything down at Clint's place?"

"No. Battery had run down. Couldn't get nuthin'."

Bill ambled in through the door. "Say! You look as white as a sheet," he remarked affably. "This here out-door life don't seem to be doin' you no good. Better get out in the sun awhile."

Steve shifted about uneasily. "Um, ah—yes, you bet,"

he groaned. "Just the thing. Ah—" His voice stuck; his throat was dry.

"Purty elegant in here," Bill quacked. "Pianner, too! Say! I ain't played a pianner in years."

"How about a little walk up to the point? I, ah— I dropped my pocketbook somewhere. I'd better go look." This was pretty bald, but it was the best excuse Steve could invent to get him out.

"Sure, sure, don't mind me. Go right along. I'll stay here and play me some hymns."

Steve glared wildly round. If he could only think of something that would amuse this moron, something he could give him to take outside and play with—

Bill sat down at the piano. "Lemme see, how does *Nellie Gray* go? Gimme the first bar. Ain't ever took a lesson, but that ain't stopped me yet. By the way, them troopers was on a false alarm." He struck some sour chords that set Steve's teeth on edge. "Said they was goin' on over west of Placid. Got a tip the gal is over there with her boy friends."

Steve wiped the sweat from his forehead.

Bill struck some more bad chords. "Must be this danged instrument ain't got her teeth in the right order," he declared, his eyes furtively searching the trailer.

"Bill, we'll walk up to the point, have a look for the pocketbook and then try some casting. Hate to waste the whole day."

"Wind's shiftin' a mite," Bill said. "Might try it on the other side of the point." He got up from the piano.

"I thought you had other things than fishin' on your mind, the way you been actin'."

"Who, me? Of course not."

"Act purty funny, I'd say."

"You're crazy. Come on, let's go!" A very definite plan for getting rid of Mr. Beaselie had taken form in his mind, and he was anxious to accomplish it.

"Hold on! I ain't seen the bathroom." Bill poked his head inside. "M'm! Looks purty flossy to me. More fer a woman than fer a man, I'd say."

"It's good for both," said Steve vaguely, selecting a rod and reel which he considered less than vital to his happiness and peace of mind.

"H'mph! You don't say. But where do you sleep? Does that thing you're settin' on unfold er somethin'? How does it work?"

"Come on, Bill! I want to get that pocketbook," Steve said flatly. He was getting desperate.

"All right, all right. What do you keep in this here closet?" Bill was in something of a dither himself, thinking of the report he was to make to Corporal Thurber.

Steve took Bill by the arm, as if he were an invalid aunt, and hurried him out.

"Say, I never knew a feller to be in such a hurry," grumbled the old man as Steve hauled him along. "Ain't even goin' to lock her up?"

Steve fumbled for his keys. The fool had unwittingly said the right thing. This would keep her safe until he came back. Plainly relieved, Steve locked the trailer door and started for the skiff. Again Bill stopped him. "You forgot your tackle box," he said.

Steve shook his head. "I'll use this spoon." He didn't propose to send his tackle box plunging to the bottom of Sand Lake. Bad enough to lose his number four rod. But these were matters about which old Bill was quite in the dark.

They walked on in a rather peculiar silence for a few moments. Then Bill stopped abruptly. "Dang it!" he snapped in seemingly great annoyance with himself, "I'm danged if I didn't forgit my oar-locks. Left 'em alongside the trailer. I'll fetch 'em. Won't take a minute."

Steve stopped and cursed. At first he'd wanted nothing better than to be separated from this inquisitive old bore—now he clung to him tenderly. "I'll go back too, Bill," he said.

"No, no, now you just hold yer horses, Steve, I'll be right back!" The old man started running for the trailer.

Steve stood still. He'd just have to bottle up his impatience and conceal his suspicions, or Bill would have altogether too much to go on. Thank God, the trailer was locked. He sat down and leaned his back against a tree, affecting elaborate boredom.

As for Bill, he edged up to the trailer window as he reached down for his locks. "Don't worry, Miss!" He croaked. "I'll have the police here before another hour."

It was no good for Gloria to pretend that she wasn't there—because she was looking him right in the eye.

The very moment he had peered inside, she was emerging from her hiding place.

She gestured hopelessly to him to go away. "No, no, no," she whispered. "Keep them waiting—don't bring them—keep them away till dark."

What else could she do but try to delay the inevitable as long as she could?

"Don't worry," hissed Bill, looking ten feet tall. "I'll pertect you. You just leave it to me."

And he picked up his oar-locks and went heroically back to Steve, whistling and staring innocently up at the sky. He'd always known he should have been a detective. This proved it. Conscience troubled him some. He hated to see Steve mixed up like this. But duty was duty. And there was a reward being offered.

*   *   *   *   *   *   *

Gloria, fuming, stood at the window and watched them until they were out of sight. Well, she gave up. She'd made such a mess of things now the only thing to do was run off to Siberia and start a new life, the way they always did in those Dostoevski novels when the corpses began to get in their way.

No, she was sick of running away. That only got other people into trouble. Better stay where you belonged and handle your own troubles right at the source.

What she really must do was think out the next step —and think it out quickly.

Albert looked at her with a stern, disapproving expression. What kind of behavior was this? Finding fault with him for tidying up a little milk, and look at the sort of things *she* did! Smudges all over her face, hair coming down.

Gloria paced back and forth, trying to think of something to do. IMPORTANT PICTURES was to blame for everything. Those buzzards! Those bloodhounds! Wait till she got her hands on them!

Albert, seeing the terrible gleam in her eyes, fell back quickly and hid under the table.

The thing to do was to get Abe Fancher to call off the hunt, of course. No more peace for Steve or her until that was done. But how could she do it?

Gloria shook her head. The only way she could think of was to find one of the troopers or deputies who were looking for her. A sudden sparkle came into her eyes. The one she let find her would collect the reward from IMPORTANT PICTURES. There would be some satisfaction in that!

But what about all the publicity? The minute word began to spread, reporters and cameramen would be down here to snap her—and Steve! It might be all straightened out after she had a chance to tell her story, but what about all the wild tales that would be told first? She knew those would be the ones that would stick in people's minds. They would be the sort of thing they *wanted* to believe.

"I've got to get *out* of here!" she said. "Got to be found somewhere else, that's clear."

She peeped out of the window. Steve and Bill were nowhere in sight.

Quick! Get out of these slacks and into a dress. She hustled her belongings into the overnight bag, and was starting for the door when she remembered Albert. It wouldn't do for him to be left behind. Incriminating evidence.

"Come on, boy! We're going for a walk."

Albert looked at her reproachfully. Walk? He'd *had* his walk. Didn't she know this was the time for his first good snooze of the day? He closed his eyes and pretended not to hear.

"Albert! Come on!"

She reached down and got him by the scruff of the neck.

What was this? An insult? So it was insults now! Albert became limp all over at the indignity.

Bag in one hand, drooping dog in her arms, Gloria pulled at the door. No good. Have to put something down. She put Albert down. He crawled back under the table. She tried the door. It wouldn't open.

Gloria rattled at the catch. Then she banged on the door. Now what on earth had he done that for? Well, she could use the window just as well.

Wait a minute! Better leave a note. Mustn't have the poor darling worrying.

She found a piece of paper and a pencil. Music paper, but that would be all right. She'd write him a song. Then nobody'd ever realize it was a note except Steve. Gloria began to think that she had been cut out for a life of crime after all. Now let's see.

Love, dove—you true— No, she'd better keep her

mind off rhymes like that, or where would she be? This would have to be one of those sad, remote, cryptic farewells. Gloria jotted down a few musical notes, sighed and then under them she wrote:

> *Though moonlight and fish*
>   *Are all I wish,*
> *There are ties that bind me,*
>   *So don't try to find me.*
> *For life is earnest, according to Longfellow,*
>   *And that is the end of my song, fellow.*
>   *Good-bye!*

"All right, Albert," she said. "We're going!"

She wrestled with a screen until she discovered how to lower it; then, taking Albert in both hands, she lifted him through the window and dropped him on the other side. The same with her overnight bag. In another moment she had wriggled through the window and was sprawling on the ground.

Albert crawled meekly under the trailer.

"Come here, boy! Come *here!*"

She dragged out the supine parcel of sullen and drooping dog, opened her bag, got out Albert's leash and fastened it to his collar. "Come *on*, Albert! We've got a lot to do."

She set off down the road, urging the reluctant dog along. He tried sitting; he tried scratching himself; he tried hauling back to sniff; but he found it was no use. He just had to keep going.

Suppose somebody saw her, Gloria thought. She'd

better put at least three miles between her and Steve before risking that.

She ventured off the road a yard or two. The going looked pretty rough. Maybe she could find a trail. Yes, and maybe she'd get lost.

She was still debating what to do when Albert began to roach his back. That was enough for her. Without a backward glance, she fled from the road.

Underbrush got in her way. She circled around it when she could or fought her way right through it. And now she noticed that these woods were full of eerie sounds, and that the light was beginning to fade.

"I'll have to get back to the road," she said. And then in gathering panic, she realized that she hadn't the slightest idea in which direction the road lay.

XIV

DOWN at the edge of the lake, the clump of bushes rustled again. A head emerged—then another head.

"Shhh!" said Corporal Thurber.

"I didn't say anything," said Higgins, the other trooper.

"That old fool is taking him out on the lake! What do you know about that?"

"H'm! I wonder if we can depend on him."

"Depend on Bill Beaselie? You bet. This New York boy is clever—he knows Bill is up to something and he's just trying to keep him from doing too much snooping. I think we'd better take another look."

"Lucky you told him that hold-up story after all."

"I'm not so sure. Haven't seen anybody so smooth in a long time."

All this while they were moving cautiously nearer to the trailer, crouching low so that they would not be seen from the lake.

When they reached the trailer they listened. Not a sound came from inside.

"I wonder—" began Corporal Thurber, frowning heavily. "Could he have done away with her?"

"My God," whispered Trooper Higgins. "A beautiful girl like that? What a terrible waste."

"Gimme a boost," said Corporal Thurber, pulling down the screen from the nearest window.

"What for? You do your own boosting pretty well. A good knock, that's what you ought to get." Trooper Higgins lifted his brother officer with many grunts and groans. "You've been gaining, sweetheart," he panted. "Don't forget to ask for her autograph!" he hissed, as the corporal's legs disappeared through the window.

The sound of hurried clumping and fumbling came from inside, also the corporal's voice. "Not in the closet. Not inside the bed. Not in the bathroom. Damn it!" His head appeared at the window. "She's not anywhere!"

"Let *me* look! They got everything in these trailers—there ought to be an extra girl around somewhere." He piled in through the window. "You and your damn Scotland Yard—look what's come of it! If you'd taken my advice we'd have closed in on the pair of 'em half an hour ago."

"Shut up! Who's the officer in charge here?"

"What was that? You'd better smile when you say it, so I'll know you're joking."

"H'mph," said Corporal Thurber, scratching his right ear. "Hey!" he cried all at once. He bent down to examine the radio. "Look here! Wire's been cut." He stared significantly up at his comrade. Then he stood up and dusted his knees.

"You get over to Boonesboro and call headquarters. Ask for two men from the barracks."

"Okay. Sure you can handle everything without me?"

"H'mph! I'll try."

Trooper Higgins wagged his finger at the corporal. "Just one thing, boy. If you see the girl, don't shoot her by mistake. It's a reward they're offering, not a bounty."

Then he climbed through the window and made for the road. He had a police car parked at the lower end of the lake.

Corporal Thurber, left alone, looked the trailer over again. Finally he climbed out through the window and had a look around outside. Probably foolish to imagine that she would be close at hand—but he had learned by experience that to be foolish was often to be right. Between six logical theories and one foolish hunch— Corporal Thurber inclined to the hunch. You couldn't expect logic from the people you were dealing with— so why apply it to them?

He started away from the trailer, carefully scanning the ground.

*   *   *   *   *   *   *

Out on the lake, Steve sat quietly in the skiff while Bill rowed it along the shore. Except for a certain glint in his eye, there was nothing to indicate the grim resolve in his mind. His brow was clear, his countenance was free of guile, and on his mouth was a gentle smile.

The more Bill quacked, the more he smiled.

"Funny I didn't see that pocketbook a-lyin' there by the tree," said Bill. "I looked there afore you did, an' I'd swear it warn't there when—"

"Eyes getting old, Bill."

"Yeh?" It was accompanied by a snort of disgust. "Ain't nothin' wrong with my seein'. . . . Well, go on and do some castin'. You was all in a pickle to get out here."

"It isn't just going through the motions that appeals to me," Steve explained. "I love fish, Bill."

"Humph!" Another snort of disgust. "The way you been heavin' and sighin' lately would make a feller think it was somethin' else than fish you was in love with. You ain't had no—no dealin's with a woman that you can't explain, have you, son? 'Cause I'm perfectly willin' fer you to explain 'em to me, if you want advice."

Steve snapped to attention. "What do you mean by that?" he demanded sharply.

"Oh—nothin', nothin' at all. But you sorta had me worried. I'd hate to see you make a mistake."

Steve managed to keep smiling. "Don't worry about me, Bill. I know what I'm doing all the time."

This silenced the old man for a few minutes.

"That there trailer o' yourn would be a dandy little place fer a honeymoon, wouldn't it?" he piped up all of a sudden.

"Yes indeed," said Steve. "Perfect." It was altogether too plain that Bill knew altogether too much. Steve decided to wait no longer. He stretched himself, laid down his rod, and slipped off his shirt.

"What you gonna do?" asked Bill. "Take a sun bath?"

"Yup," said Steve, peeling off his slacks and appearing in his shorts.

"Thought you was gonna take a bath in the lake," gabbled Bill. "But I guess you don't have to, with that there squirt-pipe you got rigged up in the trailer. He, he, he!"

"He, he," echoed Steve. Standing up all of a sudden, he dived into the lake, giving the skiff a terrific heave.

"Hey! Hi! Look out! Hey!" yelled Bill. But it was too late—the skiff went over, the water came pouring in, and Bill tumbled in with a huge, wet splash.

As for Steve, he was already ten yards away, and gaining momentum with every racing stroke.

"Hi! What's the idee?" bawled the moistened Mr. Beaselie, emerging to cough and splash. He splattered around until he got one hand on an oar. The skiff— alas!—was floating rapidly out into the lake. He shook his bony fist toward the sky. "I'll git you fer this! I'll git you if it takes forty years!"

Steve, climbing up on shore, turned and waved farewell. His voice came faintly to Bill from a distance:

"Don't—catch—cold!"

And he was gone, running swiftly among the trees.

*   *   *   *   *   *   *

Deep in a thicket, Gloria paused for breath. Her legs and arms were scratched; her face was smudged with dirt and battered with the blows of dead branches she kept running into before she saw them; she had cobwebs in her hair and mud on her dress. Anyone seeing her now would hardly believe she was the great and glamorous singing star of IMPORTANT PICTURES, INC., with marcelle by Antoine, eyelashes by

Athenée d'Ys, gowns by Adrienne, ensemble by Rosette, and smile by request of a whole battery of earnest photographers.

With her she had the wreck of a dog, with cockleburs and brambles in his hair.

"This won't do," she said firmly. "They'll take me for a tramp, if I get to civilization before I'm scratched to death."

A cloud of mosquitoes whined and stung at her; and a squadron of those maddening flies that buzz round and round your head when you are so rash as to go into the woods buzzed round and round hers.

"What I'll do to Moe!" she groaned. "Wait till I get my hands on him—just wait!"

The thought of what she would do to Moe gave her enough courage to stagger on.

Suddenly her heart leaped, and she stopped. Was that the sound of a motor? She would have sworn it was. She stood listening while the minutes passed—but all she heard now was the whine of wings and the rustle of little animals she could not see.

"Come on, boy," she said to Albert. "Porterhouse steak!"

Albert scowled, and limped after her. She had taken off the leash, because it kept getting tangled up in the brush or wound round trees.

On and on she trudged, thinking of what she would do to Moe. She had tried thinking of Steve at first, but that made her feel weak, so she put him resolutely out of her mind. He was probably cursing her this minute for being the biggest nuisance that had ever come into his life.

Gee, he was sweet! She stopped and leaned against a tree. "What am I doing?" she said. "Where am I going?" She stumbled on. Duty. A job to tackle.

Suddenly Albert, barking madly, leaped off among the trees in pursuit of some forest creature—probably smaller than himself.

"Albert! Come here!"

"Burr-rurr-rurr-rurr-rurr-rurr!" shrieked Albert, and went faster.

Gloria stamped her foot, and got it scratched in a clump of wild blackberry. "Albert! Al-bert!"

Albert was yelping like mad—his voice was far off now, in the direction they had come.

Gloria wanted to cry. Why had she ever tried to make a gentleman out of Albert? He would ruin her and her plans. She started back after him, and then stopped. Let him go back to the trailer! It would be a sign to Steve that she'd be returning soon.

And setting her chin stubbornly, she plodded on.

XV

STEVE came charging through the woods like a wild man. No more Sand Lake for him! In a couple more minutes he'd be in the car and pulling out of here—with the sweetest girl in the world for company, too. A glimpse of the trailer resulted in a fresh burst of speed that carried him to the door in a hurry.

But what was this? Why was that screen pulled down?

It stopped him in his tracks. Then, whipping out his keys, he rushed inside—only to find himself quite alone.

Where was she?

He called to her—guardedly at first, and then louder and louder. There was no answer. Slowly it began to dawn on him that she was gone.

For a minute or two he just stumbled round and round, like a stricken squirrel.

Could those troopers have come back here again, and—

He began cursing himself for going off like that while she was in danger.

Then he saw the sheet of music paper, lying carelessly on a chair. He picked it up and read what she had written.

A puzzled frown appeared on his brow. Then a look of pain. *Ties that bind,* eh?

So that was why she had run out on him. Steve felt the old chill in his bones again.

No, that wasn't fair. A girl like that didn't run out—she stuck. Look at that chin. Look at those eyes.

All right, look at them—if you could find them.

Misery, the old mother of all the sorrows, rose up in Steve and filled him full. Through all his arteries and veins the terrible poison ran. In a jam at the Carioca Club. Ducked into his trailer. In a jam here. Ducked out of the trailer.

What to do now? Get drunk, forget it, laugh it off. *Don't try to find me,* eh? Very well, if that was how she felt about it. Anyway, she'd run out just in time. Trust her for that.

"I'd better get the hell out of here," said Steve. "This is all too much for me. Carioca Club, kidnapping, cops, and now she just walks off and leaves me."

He knew he was being a fool to blame her for anything she had done—but when he was hurt and confused he couldn't help being like this. He'd offered to help her—but she'd just decided that he was no use.

Kidnapping! If that was so, the woods would be swarming with cops, and reporters would be dropping off the trees like October leaves after a frost.

Steve began to feel the frost himself.

Still—maybe she was right. It might be extremely embarrassing for her to be found with him. After all, what did he really know about her?

Just that he loved her.

Loved her? Loved a *woman?*

Steve climbed into his car and snapped on the ignition. When in doubt, act. That's what *women* did.

Well, he could do the same. Just as he started the car, the bushes rustled, and Albert came whisking gaily toward the trailer, an atavistic glow in his eyes.

So she had abandoned the pup, too!

Really, she was getting to be a regular abandoning woman. Well, this gave Albert and him a lot in common.

Smiling sourly, Steve reached down and picked Albert up by the scruff of the neck.

"Welcome, brother," he said, and started the car.

XVI

IN the innermost sanctum of the New York offices of
IMPORTANT PICTURES, INC., little Abe Fancher
tramped back and forth on a fine old rug whose dull
tones glowed richly in the watery light of afternoon—
tramped steadily and methodically as though he were
one of those mysterious people who are hired by the
hour to walk and walk until they have worn the thread
of centuries into the pattern of today. In his mouth was
a neglected cigar; on his chin was an abandoned stub-
ble; over his eyes there was a glaze.

Absently he tossed the cigar away; absently he reached
into his pocket for another; put it in his mouth; forgot
it.

A discreet knock came at his door, and a timid waiter
entered with a tray full of covered dishes.

Abe didn't see him; he just went on walking. The
waiter set the dishes carefully and silently on a table,
and then stood there.

Finally he spoke. "Mr. Fancher," he murmured.
"Your lunch again."

Abe shook his head. "Go away," he groaned.

The waiter bowed and started out. "Just a minute!"
Abe growled, and stopped walking long enough to
examine the array of dishes. "H'mph! Is this food for a

sick man? Could I eat quail the way I feel in my stomach?" Absently he bit at a stalk of celery.

"Shall I take it away, sir?"

"Take it away? Certainly you should take it away," Abe groaned, picking up an olive.

"Very well, sir." The waiter began arranging the dishes on the tray. Abe started to walk again.

"Anything more, sir?" asked the waiter, starting out.

"What's that? More? Yes! Bring me some ice."

"Yes, sir. Certainly, sir. In a—in a highball glass, sir?"

"What?" barked Abe, seizing an anchovy canapé. "No, in a bag."

"In a bag, sir?"

"A bag, a cap, a hat!" cried Abe, pointing to his head. "I want to wear it!"

"Oh! Yes indeed, Mr. Fancher. At once."

Left alone again, Abe wolfed the anchovy canapé, sighed, licked his lips, and stopped walking to stare at a fine stuffed tarpon on the wall. Every time he came around to this side of the room he looked at that tarpon. It got on his nerves. Fish, fish, fish! *He* never wanted to hear or see anything more of fish! All round the walls were reminders of his ancient love for the noble sport of angling—photographs of salmon leaping falls, of bass and pike, of speckled trout—reminders of happy, carefree days that were probably gone forever now.

He pressed a button—a secretary entered.

"Take it away!" cried Abe, waving toward the stuffed tarpon.

"Yes, sir," the secretary said. "Where shall I take it to?"

"Where? Where? Anywhere. No, wait a minute!" The ghost of a grin passed across Abe's face, and disappeared. "Take it to Mr. Wurtzberg's apartment and hang it up over his bed. Tell him I sent it as his Thought for Today."

Abe began once more to walk.

All day long people had been calling up to tell him that the Eskimos were waiting for the word to make themselves quaint in preparation for the mighty epic of the salmon industry; that the special train was waiting to start for Canada; that the sixty-five hundred assorted extras to furnish atmosphere had been rounded up; that the Curator of Ichthyology at the Museum of Natural History had finished his special treatise upon the lives, loves and special habits of the family of Salmonidae; that the elaborate costumes for the leads had been lost in transit; that they had been found again, but that they seemed to be the wrong costumes, since they consisted entirely of medieval chain mail; and so on and on and on.

But not a single word about Gloria that had come to anything—only the usual batch of letters giving advice, warning, or sympathy, with a few threats from cranks and one or two faked confessions to make it more maddening.

It was in the midst of this most unhappy state of affairs that Abe's super-special telephone, the one reserved entirely for messages of the very highest importance, rang once, rang twice, and was about to ring a third time when three secretaries appeared in the door of his office and gestured excitedly toward it. "Mr. Fancher, Mr. Fancher! They've found a positive clue!"

Not for nothing was little Abe known throughout the picture industry as the man of instant decisions (and even more instant regrets—but let nothing more be said of that). At this moment he showed his true stature as an executive.

"Answer it, Miss Everhard. Take down what she gets, Miss Mullowney. Listen in on the message, Miss Greeley. Let me have it if it's important."

He walked up to the phone and waited. At the fifth word spoken by Miss Everhard, he reached out his hand. "*I'll* take it!" he said.

As he listened he gestured wildly to Miss Everhard. "Tell Schimkin to come in here. Get Wurtzberg. Yes! Hello, Sergeant. What's that?"

The voice at the other end of the wire quacked faintly in his ear. "We have just established a positive link," it said. "No, just a clue." (This in answer to Abe's frantic interruption.) "At the moment the missing star is still—er—is still missing. Also the abductor. But one of our men has located a green trailer, parked at Sand Lake. Albany Police Headquarters confirms the fact that it corresponds with the trailer in which traffic officer O'Boyle states he saw the woman closely resembling Miss Newcombe last Wednesday. No—he cannot swear it was Miss Newcombe, but he states that he got a good look at the woman through the trailer window and he believes it was she. Troopers are being despatched to comb all roads and woods in the vicinity. Sheriff Thompson is forming a posse at Boonesboro. Would suggest Federal men in plane equipped with pontoons would be advisable. . . ."

Abe, his ear glued to the receiver, was gesturing like a windmill now—if a windmill may be said to gesture. Underlings were running through the outer offices; excited voices were calling and being answered by other excited voices; the words of the girl at the switchboard crackled like electric sparks. "Headquarters—one moment—Federal Investigator Henderson, please—Plane equipped with special pontoon landing gear to be chartered for immediate use, party of six—Mr. Wurtzberg, please—can't be disturbed? This is important—what's that? Yes, it's IMPORTANT PICTURES too, but I mean it's also *very* important—"

The busy voices went on, in gathering crescendo.

*   *   *   *   *   *   *

For a long time Steve just drove any old way and didn't care where he was going. When a road crossed the one he was on, he took it, just to be perverse. He climbed enormous hills, dived into pale misty valleys, swerved off sometimes into brush, hit a boulder at the edge of a bridge and got his fender banged up—which made him feel good—and all the time he growled and snarled to himself like the sourest old pessimist of The I'm Against It Club.

Wonder how she was doing? Must be well on her way by now. He shook his head in disgust. A hell of a thing to do, that was. The more he thought of it the less he thought of it. He guessed he'd been a fool, all right.

That was the way with women. You couldn't trust 'em. Sighing like the wind in March, he drove miserably on.

And with eyes like that, too! And a voice like an angel's. Good enough for something a lot better than night-club singing—

Oh, to hell with that. Stop thinking about her. He'd just made a fool of himself again.

But this time he would swear a terrible and solemn oath never to trust any woman, no matter how beautiful. Never again. Not on your life. He was cured. He was *really* cured.

Steve lifted his right hand in the air, dropped it, and sighed. Wonder if she was thinking about him.

*　　*　　*　　*　　*　　*　　*

High over the great hills, in the fair unclouded sky, a tiny speck appeared. Thus it is, in the clear untroubled calm of life, that trouble so often comes. At first it is no larger than a speck, and the unfortunate victim-to-be pays it no heed. But it grows—it swells—it expands—and before he knows it, that first infinitesimal mote has become a blot—a smooch—an ineradicable and mountainous lump in the midst of his day, so huge that it hides all else from the eyes, stifles the breath, deafens the ears, makes the mouth dumb, and casts woe and confusion upon the mind.

Thus with this speck, this blot, this smooch. Nor did

it stay a smooch either, but grew larger and larger still. With its increase in size came a steady augmentation of the sound which emanated from it—first a hum, then a buzz, then a louder and louder roar, until it filled the air and swallowed all other sounds except the little piping cries of the inhabitants of Boonesboro, who came running out to see what was going to happen, and hoping, undoubtedly, that it was going to be something rich and big—something fine to look at, something extremely awkward for somebody because that made it more dramatic, and something exceedingly loud and public, because that made it much more fun.

So, to the accompaniment of the said roaring, and amid the great expectations of those who watched its arrival, the plane bearing Mr. Abraham Fancher, Mr. Moe V. Wurtzberg and several official representatives of the Department of Justice, swooped rapidly down upon the waters of Sand Lake, coasted along on its pontoons, sending up a beautiful white spray, and came to rest only one yard and three quarters from the police launch waiting to receive its passengers.

They were swiftly and expertly transferred from the plane to the launch; and in a few minutes were on dry land and ready for the fulfillment of their mission— about which the gaping watchers were extremely positive but distressingly at variance—though the consensus of opinion seemed to be that it was either a Congressional investigation, the initiation of a new Public Works Project, or the solution of the great kidnapping case at last.

"We bin askin' fer that there new post office long enough!" sagely opined a bristling greybeard, wagging his head—and, of course, the beard with it. " 'Bout time we had some action!"

"Huh!" piped up a towheaded kid. "If them's Guv'-ment men, I hope they're here to do some shootin', in-stead o' buildin'."

An avid knot of citizens trailed the party of distin-guished men as it headed for Justice Hockenberry's garage, filling station, funeral parlor and general store.

But the party did not enter the Justice's establishment —instead, it debouched into a pair of cars drawn up before his door, and before Boonesboro quite knew what was happening, it had disappeared in a cloud of dust.

"Let's go see Sheriff Thompson!" cried a disappointed voice. "He may know what's up."

They started for the sheriff's office. They had not quite reached it when one of their number cried: "Hi! There's another plane comin'!"

The hum of the second plane swelled to a roar as it swooped down. Boonesboro's excited citizenry went hurrying back to the lake front.

If the first amphibian had seemed important, this one (special pride of the *Comet*, New York's most pros-perous tabloid) far surpassed it—for out of it came leaping and gesticulating a band of news-hawks and photographers, with a smart-looking tear-jerker in their midst whose column was syndicated from coast to coast.

No sooner had they landed their nervous feet upon

solid soil than they set to work with their cameras and tongues—collecting atmosphere, spreading excitement, sprinkling joy upon the grateful citizens, who shoved closer and closer when these great arrivals congregated in a group, and trailed them like a comet's tail when they went seething and swishing through the village with their fiery news:

"The kidnapper has been traced to Sand Lake! The missing star has almost been found! The kidnapper is a millionaire's son! It's the most romantic crime of the century!"

Let the *Times* and the others take their story through the A. P. if they wanted to. Not the *Comet*. "Spare no expense" had been the final word—and this bunch didn't have to be told twice. Where could they hire cars, guides—who had a telephone—where was the nearest Western Union office?—

And so on, and on. The citizens rose nobly to what was asked and expected of them—pouring out columns of atmosphere, conjecture, rumor, surmise, and misinformation, which included six detailed descriptions of the kidnapper, all widely different, and fourteen reminiscences of events which had no connection whatever with the crime but which were offered as valuable contributions, occupied the attention of the more receptive newsmen on their way from the lake to the center of the village, where they were met with the news that Sheriff Thompson was organizing a posse.

Night was rapidly coming down—and it was going

to be a bad one. Especially for the kidnapper, when they got him.

"Come on, boys! Every man out for the posse! We'll scour the woods from here to Truro!"

There hadn't been as much excitement in Boonesboro since the War.

XVII

GLORIA was really frightened—and quite lost. For a long time she had given up trying to find her way at all, and just went blindly on.

At first she had dreaded the dark, but she gave up minding it after it came. It wasn't so bad—it was the little sounds she heard around her that bothered her. There weren't wolves in these woods, were there? Or bears? If only she hadn't run away from Steve! She shivered.

For an hour or two, perhaps even more, she had lain under a tree and slept from sheer exhaustion. When she woke up she saw the moon shining palely down at her, and that gave her courage. After all, it was such a friendly looking moon—and it made her think of last night—they had been so gay with their music.

Better not think of that—she didn't want to cry. She had never been good at crying—it hurt a lot, and didn't seem to help any. She had always envied the people who were adept at it.

Suddenly, without expecting it at all, she stumbled onto a path that wound among the great trees. She felt like crying then, but from sheer relief. But she laughed instead, and started walking faster.

It wasn't long before the path led to a little road—and gathering all her scattered forces, she trudged grimly down it. If she met anyone, she would just speak up and say who she was. And she would ask to be taken to the nearest house, where she could lie down and go to sleep.

No, she couldn't do that. She had to reach Abe or Moe somehow, and get them to call off this horrible farce. She wondered why on earth she hadn't done it before. Why had she run out on them in the first place?

Oh yes—fish.

Fish?

She didn't mind fish any more. There was a lot to be said for fish. There was even more to be said for fishermen. Or for one of them at least.

Suddenly she heard the noise of someone thrashing about among the brush. She knew it was a man, because she heard him talking to himself.

She ran to the other side of the road and crouched down in some bushes, listening with rapidly beating heart. The individual seemed to be coming her way. Oh, if she'd only stayed with Steve, that paragon, that prince of men! A bulky form separated itself from the darkness. She caught the shimmer of a shield on his coat. Police, she told herself.

All her high resolves fled from her. Give herself up? She couldn't, she wouldn't, she just wasn't going to! It was too ridiculous—she'd feel like a fool for the rest of her life.

And besides, she was too frightened. This gloomy road, alone with this man—how did she know what kind of a cop he was? She waited until he had tramped on out of sight and hearing, and then she tiptoed softly out and began to run. Before she had taken three steps she heard the man rushing back.

"Hi!" he shouted. "Hold up there! You stop or I'll shoot!"

Gloria's heart did a hop-skip-and-jump—and she sped on faster than ever.

Ten minutes later she reached a cross-road. She took it—because away off in the distance she could see a faint glow from the window of a little house. Behind her sounds of pursuit had dimmed.

"A house—" she gasped.

It was about time, too—she had begun to wonder if anybody at all lived in this part of the world. Her spirits revived tremendously. At least she didn't have to go up to a strange bulky man with a badge in the middle of a deserted road. She could sit down on a chair now, and see the people she was going to tell her story to.

"Well, here I go," she said, and marched up to the shack and knocked on the door.

"Who's there?" called a voice from somewhere inside—a woman's voice.

H'm! That's a dandy question. Who am I, anyway? Gloria felt stumped for a reply. But she had no need to answer, for the door opened a crack and an old woman peered out. After eyeing Gloria in silence for a few moments, the woman opened the door a little wider.

"You Zeke Hawkins' niece from the city!"

"No, I'm sorry but I'm—somebody else. I'm lost. Would you let me come in and rest? I need—"

"Why, child, you look a perfect sight!" said the woman, opening the door wide. "Wherever have you come from at this time of night?"

"Oh—just from over that way," said Gloria, gesturing vaguely.

"Come in, gal, come in! Come and set!"

Gloria stumbled over the threshold, fell into a chair in the kitchen, and just sat there, in a daze of fatigue and hunger.

Suddenly the old woman looked at her hard. "I swear, child, you ain't that kidnapped actress? Woods is full of people huntin' fer somebody like you."

Gloria began weakly to laugh. She had felt so alone in the woods.

"Land o' heaven, dear, you gave me such a shock! I shouldn't wonder if this brings on a stroke, I shouldn't." She fetched a basin of warm water and sat down beside Gloria. "Jest reach me that towel and I'll bathe your pore face." She was panting with excitement. "Phew! Won't Henry be surprised when he gits back from the posse and finds it was *me* who found you! Let me look at you, child."

"But how—why—how could you know about me?" stammered Gloria.

"How? Whole country's swarmin' with people who're lookin'. Every man as ain't drunk or laid up is out gadding through the woods on t'other side of the lake.

Figgered a feller in one of these trailer houses had run off with yuh—"

The other side of the lake? It made Gloria realize how far she had come. But she dismissed that in a sudden constriction of the heart. What must be happening to Steve? She began to talk very fast. "Listen—you must help me get to a telephone right away! And to the police! It's a very urgent—"

"Now, child, don't excite yourself." The old woman put an arm around her. "You're goin' to be fine, you see if you ain't. Telephone just a little piece down the road at Mr. Fancher's estate. I'll git my shawl and trot over with you."

Gloria stared at her. "At *whose* estate?"

"Mr. Fancher. Big feller in the movies, they say. I guess he'll be glad to let you use his phone. I heard from Billy Brown, in here this afternoon to git Henry, that Mr. Fancher was very anxious to find you. . . . What *have* you been up to, child?"

Gloria came out of her daze, and began to laugh. "Just going round in circles," she said weakly. "Just waiting for Fate to come along and lead me back where I started."

She sat down and began to laugh harder. So that was where she had heard the name of Sand Lake! She remembered now—in Abe's office!

Well, she gave up. Hollywood to New York—and right into a nest of them. New York to Sand Lake—it was perfect, it was like those things that happen to a friend of a friend of your old Uncle George, who swears to the truth of his story and hardly believes it himself. People running around the world to get away from each other—and passing on a street in Cairo—meeting in the same pastry shop in Bond Street—using each other's telephone in Sand Lake.

The old woman looked at Gloria and shook her head. "Well, I always wanted to meet one of you famous stars, seen a few of you in pictures over to the county seat, but I swear, child, you're jest like plain folks. Nothin' different about you at all. Remind me of my datter Mildred when she was a little thinner than she is now. Had five babies, she did—sort of took on flesh, and all." Gabbling innocently, and with as much naturalness as if Gloria had been her daughter in fact, Grandma Dexter took her shawl and held out her arm.

"Well, my dear, let's you and me start. I know you want to rest, but it'll be more relaxin' after you've done what you want to do. Ain't that so? That's the way it is with me. When I've got somethin' on my mind, you can't do a thing with me till I've had my way. Now you look a mite stubborn yourself—so I shouldn't wonder if you'd be the same as me."

"I'm stubborn, all right," said Gloria. "You wait and see how stubborn I am."

She was making a firm resolve to herself all this while. One good thing was going to come of all this—those cannibals had offered a reward. Well, this kindly old soul was going to have it—or by all that was holy, she would run off again.

"Here we are," said the old woman, pointing up a

hill to a handsome log house that seemed to ramble in all directions. "Mr. Fancher's place. Lodge, he calls it. . . . That's the edge of the lake you see down there. Private beach, he has—can't bathe with common folks. Well, I'll leave you at the door. I've got my bread rising, so I'll have to be getting back."

Gloria smiled down at her. "Thanks so much for being kind to me. I'll see you soon—and I'll have a present for you." She patted the old woman's arm. "I'll be all right," she said, and knocked on the door.

There was silence for a moment—then the sound of approaching footsteps. Gloria peeped through the glass—and almost swooned. Moe! How had he ever got here? She didn't know—she'd given up trying to figure out the reasons for catastrophes, but just assumed that they would occur.

"Good evening, Moe," she said softly as the door opened.

A wan, pale, harassed face appeared; two weary eyes stared out at her; and then Moe's jaw dropped.

"I was just passing by, and thought I'd drop in," said Gloria demurely. "I heard you were sort of looking for me."

"Whuh—whuh—whuh—" said Moe.

"Now just relax, please," said Gloria, taking him by the arm and leading him to a comfortable rocking chair. "Because you're going to have a lot to do in a minute. Where's Abe? I suppose he's right in the next room?"

"Abe? Abe? Listen, Gloria, what's the meaning of

this? Who took you? What did you do? Where did you come from? Abe! Oh, Jenkins! Wake Mr. Fancher. Tell him the—tell him the fugitive, I mean the missing captive—"

Gloria heard more footsteps. She set her jaw. Now for it. A door opened, and two servants appeared, blinking. Another door opened, and Corporal Thurber came tumbling out, buttoning up his tunic. His eyes popped at sight of her. "You!" he cried. "Old Bill was right after all. But—but how'd you get here?"

Before Gloria could frame an answer a familiar step sounded above—and little Abe, yawning hugely, in dressing gown and pajamas, came scrambling down the stairs. "Gloria! Gloria! My goodness! Who found you? The rescue party left two hours ago for the entirely hopeless purpose of checking up again. We were about ready to give up. What happened? Who did it?"

"It's you who ought to be telling *me* things," Gloria said. "But we'll skip that for the moment. First, I want you to call off your army. Then you've got to kill any publicity that has developed concerning—"

"Gloria, baby! My God, I thought I'd never see you again!" Abe wiped the tears from his eyes. He danced around her like a rejuvenated poodle. "But listen, should I kill publicity when it's the biggest build-up a star has ever got in the history of—"

"Look, Abe—I can still run," said Gloria, getting up and tottering weakly toward the door.

Moe and Abe and five staring people snatched for her.

"All right, all right, anything you say!" cried Abe. "Would I deny you anything? Listen, Gloria—"

"Hurry, Abe, please! There's something important you've got to do for me. It's about a—a man."

Abe quivered, as if a slight shock had passed through him. He stared at her. That voice—he'd always known there had been something lacking in it, beautiful as it was—the tremolo, that was what it never had possessed.

And here it was. Abe felt a warm glow in his chest. He sat down beside Gloria and took her hand. "Tell me all about him, baby," he said. "By the way, Gloria, what is it you have been really up to before the explanations begin in earnest?"

The wan and wasted Moe leaned forward. "Yes, Gloria, for the love of Mike what are you doing out in this God-forsaken hole?"

Abe glared him to silence. "Gloria, what have you been doing?"

Gloria looked him in the eye. "I've been fishing," she said.

XVIII

STEVE had never been able to sulk very long—it made him sick, it made his head ache, he didn't like it. So after some hours of morbid brooding under some particularly gloomy trees, he gave it all up and climbed back into the car with Albert. He felt a great relief as soon as he stepped on the gas; and more and more of it as he threaded his way back along the roads by which he had come.

This would lead him back to the lake—and he was glad. He felt the same compulsion, he supposed, that murderers felt in returning to the scene of the crime. And in a way he had been trying to commit a murder —for in scoffing at his feeling for Gloria and in trying to smother it under a mound of gloomy thoughts he had been trying to kill something that was very much alive, and wanted to live. That it drove him back now was a sign that it could not be smothered, no matter how hard he tried.

How gentle she was! How good and kind—and as beautiful as the best of her qualities. Steve hoped she was sorry she had gone.

He could have helped her. Nobody else would have done as much as he wanted to do. Being a man, he was hurt most at the fact that she hadn't seemed to need his strength. There is a limit to resourcefulness and independence—in a woman. How is a man to *feel* like one if the woman he loves is perfectly able to protect herself? What is *he* to do, anyway? Putter round in the kitchen with the cups and saucers? Take up knitting? Study embroidery?

He reached the clearing by the lake—the moon would be bright tonight; there wasn't a cloud in the sky, and the water glistened like silk. (Like her dress.)

Sighing still more, he came to a stop, and got out of the car. Then, as Albert jumped down and began to scratch about in the dirt, he sat down on the running-board and leaned his chin upon his hand.

Well, here he was. Nothing to do, not even any fishing—so that he should be perfectly free to compose a dozen songs and at least three-quarters of a concerto.

Music? Bah!

That made him think of how her voice had sounded last night. He hadn't realized how happy he'd been. The whole thing seemed a far-away, impossible dream. The world, these woods, the moonlight, the happy chirping sounds of forest creatures getting ready to go to sleep, and of others equally ready to stay awake and keep everybody else awake too—all seemed empty, barren, meaningless, absolutely no good.

How empty the night was! And how terribly empty it was going to be!

Steve let his head sink lower—it needed two hands to support it now.

It was at this moment that the sound of a car came to his ears. Of two cars—of several cars—of motorcycles. The noise grew rapidly louder. He didn't move. The glow of headlights ran along the trees, glared in his eyes, grew brighter. There was the sound of many voices—and he found himself surrounded by excited men, carrying shotguns and earnestly demanding to know what he had done with the girl.

Well, here it was. Steve sighed, and stood up. Anyway, the night wasn't empty any more. That was something.

A fat, sweating man with a long, firm nose and a prominent jaw elbowed his way through the crowd, dragging a familiar figure along with him. The familiar figure proved to be Bill Beaselie.

"Well, is that him?" demanded the fat man.

"Yup," said Bill, his thin voice unsteady with excitement; "that's him. The girl's in the trailer. I talked to her—jest as I told you."

Steve glanced at him reprovingly. This was too funny to lose his temper about it. "Bill, I never thought a Beaselie would turn traitor. Benedict Arnold Beaselie—"

"No you don't!" old Bill cackled; "you can't abuse me that way! I was fer you—tried to make yuh see the error of your ways, but when you dumped me into the lake you went too far. Besides, I can use that reward jest as well as the next feller."

"Reward?" Maybe this should be taken seriously after all.

"Five thousand dollars!" snapped the fat man with

the long nose. "I'm the sheriff of this county. You're the man we want. We know you, all right."

Steve felt the most hideous boredom weighing down on him. He wanted to yawn, and if his father hadn't trained him always to be polite, even to the most insufferable people, he would have gaped in the fat man's face.

"Well," he said vaguely. "I don't know *you*, sir. But make yourselves at home. Come in, come in. My, er—establishment is a bit snug, but you'll find a snack for yourselves in the ice-box. If I'd known you were coming I'd have laid a few extra plates."

The visitors didn't seem to like this. They made quite a lot of noise. After all, a posse is a posse. It doesn't want to decompose, disintegrate and desiccate into a mere collection of self-conscious people who have suddenly had their reason for being together taken away from them.

At this moment another car arrived. It disgorged half-a-dozen men and a girl. Their arrival acted like a powerful tonic on the posse's sagging morale. Almost instantly the flash bulbs began to pop. Employing a combination of the Minnesota shift and the Notre Dame flying wedge, these earnest young men and the equally earnest young woman who accompanied them made it first down on the first play.

Steve blinked as a photographer held a camera up to him and set a bulb off almost in his face. Presently a whole series of pops and glares ringed him in. He tried to push the picture-snatchers away, but clinging to his arm he found a girl with a low, cooing voice, wanting to know all about his love-nest out here in the wilds, and his impressions of American womanhood.

"Who are you?" Steve groaned, to this strange female.

"Me? I'm Anne Darling of the New York *Comet*. You know, Anne Darling?" She was sure he knew. "It's a pleasure to meet a great appreciator of women like you, Mr. Greene. Just what was your purpose in abducting Miss Newcombe, the lucky girl? What a blond beast you are, Mr. Greene. Tell me, does a feeling come over you sometimes—"

"Hey! Pipe down, Anne!" cried one of the photographers. "All we can get is your mouth. Give us a chance."

But Miss Darling's saga was indefinitely postponed by Sheriff Thompson, who at this point seized Steve roughly by the arm. "You come inside with me. Stay right around here, boys! Jake, you watch the door."

Steve allowed himself to be shoved into the trailer. What the hell? Life was no good anyway.

"You got anything on you?" asked the Sheriff, frisking him for a gun or other deadly weapon, and finding none.

"We're going to ask you some questions," the fat man informed him, indicating the several solemn-faced men who had followed him inside.

Before the questions could be put, however, a brisk young man crowded past Jake, at the door, and with alert, sharp eyes examined, tabulated, catalogued and classified everything inside the trailer in a series of lightning glances. They rested most sharply and acutely upon Steve, and set to work classifying him.

Steve disliked this young man very much. He didn't mind Sheriff Thompson; the old fool was probably all right, and after all, none of this was his fault. Didn't the dolt realize that all the troubles men had were the fault of women? He began to feel angry at Gloria again.

"Let's talk about women," Steve said. "I bet you don't get treated right at home, either of you. You look all pecked up."

The young man with the beady eyes looked quizzically at Steve. "Sheriff Thompson, let me ask this man a question or two. I've got a flash—"

"Okay," said the sheriff, relaxing on the piano bench. Obviously this young man was someone whose acumen he respected.

"Now, Mr. Greene," began the young man, "I'm Win Winfield, of the *Comet*. You know, 'Crash-With-a-Smash' Winfield?"

Steve looked at him blankly. Strange, how these people were all so confident he had heard all about them.

"You read my column?" asked Winfield.

"No—"

"You've heard me on the radio?"

"No—"

"Well, it doesn't matter," snapped Winfield. "Maybe I've been misinformed. But let's get down to cases. Things look bad for you. Still, it's perfectly possible that you are entirely innocent of any crime. We are here to get the facts—and Gloria Newcombe."

"I see," said Steve dryly. "Well, I'm hungry, and so is my dog. Do you mind if I just putter about while you get your facts and whoever this lady is you seem to want?"

"Just a minute, Mr. Greene. The facts about you are known. The point is, what ones are going to appear in the papers? What facts are going to settle your status with the law?"

"You tell me," said Steve. "Do you like ham on rye?"

"In the first place, how do you happen to have hidden yourself in the woods for three days with a missing movie star? How does it happen that you—"

"A missing what?" cried Steve.

Mr. Winfield smiled quickly, and then looked very stern. "I suppose you never go to the movies?" he asked gently.

Steve's head had begun to swim. He thought he had seen her somewhere! On a poster, probably. "That's right," he said. "I never do."

The *Comet's* ace man lit a cigarette with a flourish, and then barked: "Where have you hidden Miss Newcombe?"

Steve barely heard him. A movie star! What a fool he'd been! He should have known she was somebody special. Still, he didn't think she fitted that type very well, either. He fastened one eye on Mr. Winfield.

"Tell me," he said, "what kind of an actress is she?"

"What kind of an actress? Do you mean to say you've never *seen* her? Do you imply that you never *heard* her? What kind of a game is this, anyway? Am I being kidded?"

"Well, I just want *your* impressions," Steve said humbly.

"*Everybody* has seen Gloria Newcombe," Crash-With-a-Smash said icily. "The most beautiful voice in pictures. And why wouldn't it be? It comes straight from the Metropolitan Opera."

Steve gulped. Then he choked. "Wha—what did you say?"

Winfield shook his head, and got sullen. "Nerts!" he exclaimed. "I'm not in this just for the human interest."

Steve was in a daze. Metropolitan! *That* was it! He knew it must be so—and he knew why he hadn't recognized her. He'd been in Europe, listening to fat old popinjays in Paris and Milan—when he could bear them—while she had been blazing her career in America. They'd missed each other on two continents, it seemed.

The faint echoes of recollection began to stir in his mind. Also, the dull ache of regret and shame. So *he* was the boy who had told her she had possibilities! *He* was the gent who had offered to coach her! Oh Lord. Oh my God. Steve buried his face in his hands.

He was so wrapped up in his bitter thoughts that the sharp young man could get no more out of him.

Steve just waved him dully away. After awhile the door of the trailer opened and a tall, quiet man entered. "I'll take this," he said to the Sheriff and Winfield. "You boys were quick, all right." He sat down opposite Steve and looked at him sternly.

"What have you to say for yourself?" he said.

Steve got more bitter still. He wanted to jump up and sock these dull, unpleasant fellows.

But no, he thought. Might as well be careful. After all, how'll the old man feel if he sees all this spattered over the papers? Got to hang on to myself. What will *Vivian* say? Oh Lord, I'll *never* get that divorce now —she'll hang on to me just to have the satisfaction of being injured and deceived.

He sighed, and came out of his trance. "Well, gentlemen, it's like this," he began. "One day I decided I wanted to get away from it all and just go fishing by myself. That's where I made my first big mistake. . . ."

"Never mind about mistakes. We'll take care of them," said the tall, quiet man. "Just answer my questions, please."

At this moment a short, thick, decisive man came into the trailer. "*I'll* handle this, men!" he said.

The three earnest investigators jumped to their feet. "Certainly, sir. We were just trying to get the essential facts," apologized the tall, quiet man.

"That's quite right, men!" said the newcomer. "Now, Mr. Greene, just answer my questions, please."

Steve smiled in spite of himself. Too bad Corporal

Thurber wasn't here. He would have enjoyed it. "No accounting for tastes," thought Steve. He wondered how many more important people were going to pop in and say: "I'll handle this!" And how much more important they were going to get. It was like some kind of dull parlor game, in which the other people asked all the questions. Not quite fair, Steve thought.

He resigned himself once more to the questions that were going to come.

"Do I guess who you are, or do you guess who I am, or are you just Napoleon?" he asked.

The new arrival didn't like this. "I'd advise you to be careful of what you say, young man. This is no joke," he snapped. "We want the facts, and we want them straight! I'm a Department of Justice agent."

Steve wondered what to say. If he did tell the true story, who would believe it? He could see the headlines —MILLIONAIRE'S SON FOUND IN NORTH WOODS WITH MISSING MOVIE QUEEN—he could see his family's faces, too—and hear their voices. Vivian's voice. He decided he'd tell these dreary fellows that he'd just given the girl a lift—didn't know who she was.

He tried to think as clearly as he could. After all, he'd have to protect her too. If she'd only trusted him! If she'd only *depended* on him! How different he'd feel! And what a lot more he would know!

Anyway, he would do his best.

XIX

SEVERAL hours later, he was still trying. The questioners, exhausted, had taken off their shirts, and sat in the trailer fanning themselves. The sharp young reporter had become an extremely dull one—the camera men had popped and flashed themselves into extinction. Steve was munching at some toast and drinking coffee—they had all had something to eat from his larder. The chief questioner had just finished his catechism for the time being, and was preparing to take Steve along with them—for further questioning.

Outside the original posse had diminished in size—all hangers-on had been sent off about their business, and only those with some kind of authority remained. It was all quite grim, and Steve was heartily tired of it.

He felt a little sick, too. It seemed clear to him that this thing Gloria had done was just a publicity stunt. What else could it possibly have been? The reporter seemed to feel the same way—and to be prepared to give it all the publicity any movie queen could desire.

Publicity stunt—and he had been prepared to help her, risk his life if she needed it. No wonder she hadn't accepted his help. That would have gummed up the whole thing. Full of miserable frustration and mental conflict, Steve munched toast and let them talk away. He was away past boredom now—past rage, revolt, past everything but a pain in his stomach and an ache in his head.

Suddenly all of them looked up. A trooper entered and saluted. It was Corporal Thurber at last. "I've got instructions to ask you Department of Justice men and Sheriff Thompson to call off this investigation," he said, breathing hard. "The lady has been found and is with her friends. The whole kidnapping story was trumped up. I have a note for you from Mr. Fancher and orders from Inspector Henderson."

After tossing this bomb-shell, Corporal Thurber stood there and looked extremely embarrassed. In fact, there was nobody in the trailer who didn't look embarrassed except Steve. No word has yet been found to describe how *he* looked.

Agent Phelps cleared his throat. "Let me see those papers," he barked. He looked as if he wanted to break the trooper's neck—and decapitate Steve. After all his careful questions! After all his delicate skill in unearthing the facts—or some of them, anyway. He snatched at the papers the trooper held diffidently out to him. Grunting, he read them rapidly through, and without a word passed them to the others.

Steve stared bleakly at all of them. Then he got up. "Well, gentlemen, it's been nice having you. But now that you've got your little mistake adjusted among yourselves would you mind very much if I start adjusting some mistakes of mine? It's very late."

*　*　*　*　*　*　*

After they had gone, he went into the bathroom and doused his head thoroughly. Then he doused it some more. God, how it ached! Anger is bad, when you can't do anything about it. Especially when it's against a woman. And when she isn't anywhere near you.

He dried his face, gave Albert some more milk, patted him on the head, went outside and looked grimly at the moon, snapped the trailer door shut, and got into the car. Then he got out again, and locked the trailer door. No passenger *this* time!

Then he started the car. Good-bye to Sand Lake. Good-bye to Bill Beaselie. Good-bye to Miss Movie Star. In a moment more he was speeding rapidly along the lake.

The car jounced and squeaked; he didn't care. He just gave it more gas.

By morning a whole *crew* of reporters would be swarming all over the place, he supposed. Vacation in the Adirondacks! A little quiet fishing! A safe retreat from the cares of the world! A refuge from women and other afflictions! Bah!

After about an hour of impossible bumpy roads that even a cow would hesitate to use for a path, Steve came to a highway. The car leaped forward.

Where he was going he didn't know, but he was going to get there in a hurry.

What ghastly country this was! Scraggly old burnt-over trees, stagnant ponds, clouds of mosquitoes—nothing but dreary swamp. Well, that was appropriate, all right. It was just like life—a miasmatic bog. The idéal place for him to camp for the night.

Turning up the first dirt road he saw, Steve drove for a few miles through the same gloomy country, hating it and glad it was hateful.

In a particularly dank and scraggly location, where no man in his right mind would ever dream of lingering, Steve grimly brought his car to a stop.

The idiotic voice of a loon came quivering eerily over the boggy land. Mosquitoes whined and stung; inside the trailer Albert lifted his nose ceiling-ward, and howled.

Wonderful! Steve got out and stood for awhile in the soggy swamp-grass, admiring the beautiful scene and slapping at mosquitoes. Ah, if Miss Movie Queen could only be here now, to share this breath-taking and most intriguing loveliness!

Steve went inside the trailer to reason with Albert. After awhile he turned on the light and sat down at the piano. What's this? Some of his music gone? He searched frantically through the tumbled sheets—yes, it was gone, all right.

Exquisite! Delicious! He wouldn't be surprised if she had used it to wrap up a pair of muddy shoes.

The only melody he had worked on recently which still seemed to be here was the one about women, and how good-for-nothing they were. Huh! She *would* leave that.

Lucky he hadn't told her he was married.

Lucky? Why lucky? What did he care, one way or

the other? He bent down and stared at the radio. You know, come to think of it, there was something very funny about all this. Just why was his set not working? It was new, and he'd tested it before starting. He felt along the back. Hey, what's this? He stooped over and twisted the set around. Aha! The wires had been cut.

Bless her little heart! What a thoughtful creature she was! He joined the ends of the wires and snapped the radio on. It worked fine.

Say! If what that damned reporter said was true, this mess must have been *broadcast!* He set to work feverishly with the dials.

*   *   *   *   *   *   *

At about this time, a car drew up in the clearing, and Gloria leaped out.

"He's *gone!*" she cried.

"What's that? Gone?" said Moe's voice—and he leaped out too.

"Oh, I'll never forgive myself!"

"Now, now, Gloria—you couldn't foresee everything, you just couldn't."

"That horrid possé! Why didn't you tell me sooner? What will we *do?*"

"Come on—it's back to Inspector Henderson for us. And then New York."

"I won't, I won't, I—"

"Now listen, Gloria, this man has a wife and family. You realize that. You've got to think of his reputation as well as yours. You've got to—"

Gloria got into the car and slumped down on the seat. "All right. I'll go," she said in a dull voice. "And I hope we have a wreck on the way. I hope we—"

Moe started the car. "Now, Gloria," he said. "Just relax. Just take it easy."

Gloria began to cry.

XX

DR. HUBERMANN, the world-famous authority on nervous disorders, tiptoed out of a darkened suite at the Waldorf Astoria, and into an ante-room. It was early in the evening of the following day.

"Yes?" whispered a wan, anxious shadow.

"H'm," observed Dr. Hubermann.

"Is she any better?" asked the shadow.

"That is the question, Mr. Wurtzberg. That is—ah—the question. Physically, she is perfectly sound. I would say, in fact, that I have never seen a finer specimen of—ah—"

"Sure, sure, all right, but what we want to know is, can she broadcast tonight or not? *That's* the question. With all the publicity she's got now, it would be a catastrophe if she wasted it. Why, this is the greatest romantic build-up a star ever had. We've especially arranged this broadcast on the Littlejohn Tabasco Hour. The sponsor's wild—the public's waiting with its tongue out—our publicity department is running itself ragged—"

"I'm sorry, Mr. Wurtzberg, but as her physician I wouldn't advise Miss Newcombe's particip—"

"Listen, I tell you it's a catastrophe! After all I've done, after—"

Another shadow came into the ante-room. "What is

this?" said the new shadow. It was Abe. "Do you mean to tell me that we are going to let the public down? It's impossible! IMPORTANT PICTURES has a responsibility to the public which it's never shirked yet. Listen, doctor—"

At this moment still another shadow spoke—but this time it was in the suite itself. "What's the trouble now?" asked a dull, tired voice—Gloria's.

"Shhh!" hissed Dr. Hubermann. "You must go right back to bed. It's nothing at all. Please don't excite yourself."

"Who said something about a broadcast?"

"Now wait a minute, Gloria, we'll tell you all about it in just a moment. Just come lie down, baby—that's a good girl."

"I'm not a good girl! I'm a *terrible* girl!"

"All right, all right, anything you say, Gloria. Take her other arm, Moe."

"I *won't* be responsible," cried Dr. Hubermann.

"All right, doc, you don't have to be. There. That's the good girl—excuse me, I mean the terrible girl. There."

"What's this broadcast? What were you talking about? You needn't think just because I've taken all that medicine I'm not perfectly alert and able to—"

"That's just what I was telling the doc, here," said Abe, perspiring earnestly. "Now listen, Gloria. . . . *You* tell her, Moe!"

The stricken Moe leaped nervously in the semi-darkness. "Who, me?"

"Well, you're her agent. What do you collect your commission for?"

"Listen, Abe, from anybody else I would't even take it—"

"H'mph. You take the dough all right. I've always admired the slick way you handled that part of the job. Now look, Gloria, it's just a matter of a little broadcast, see? Explain it, Moe."

The unhappy agent mopped his brow. "Well, it's like this, honey. We want everybody to know you're all right, see? They're anxious. They're worried. They just can't bear to miss a heart-beat. We want you just to say a few words, understand? And then maybe sing a couple of—what did you say?"

Gloria spoke very quietly. "I didn't say anything—yet."

"Oh! I thought you did. Well, now look—you can broadcast in a private room—lying down. How about that for convenience and consideration? We've been working out the arrangements with the studio all afternoon. We— What did you say? Oh, pardon me. What *do* you say? Now remember, Gloria, we've done a lot for you. We've worn ourselves to the bone."

Gloria sat up in bed. "I've got just one word to say," she said.

Moe and Abe shuffled anxiously. Dr. Hubermann bent over her. "Now, Miss Newcombe, no excitement, please."

"It's *yes!*" said Gloria. "Now run along and don't bother me until it's time to go on the air."

Moe jumped. "Did you say yes? Gloria, do you mean you actually will do it?"

"Why of course, darling! I'd do *anything* to please you!"

Later, out in the hall, Abe and Moe faced each other in dull amazement. Gloria had said yes; she'd actually been eager to say yes. It was incredible.

"Moe—you don't think her mind is going—er—something?"

Moe could only shake his head. "Search me," he sighed. "For once I don't even think. I just pray."

*   *   *   *   *   *   *

Deep in some rather unpleasant woods, though not nearly so bad as those in which he had spent the previous night, Steve was moodily washing the supper dishes and listening to the radio.

Albert, capaciously fed, was lying on the bed in the midst of an elegant snooze.

Steve was having a terrible bout of self-pity. Look at me, he was thinking. Getting on toward thirty. Never meant anybody any harm, always tried to treat people right, and look what I get. Have to hide away from the world in a swamp. Played for a fool by the only girl I ever cared anything about. She's probably laughing at me right now. As if I care!

"It is our special pleasure, ladies and gentlemen," came the voice of the announcer on the Tabasco Hour program, "to introduce to you now one of the greatest living stars of opera and the silver screen—a girl whose name is on everybody's lips, and who, I am happy to say, is safe and sound, in good health, and has never looked more beautiful than she does this moment. Ladies and gentlemen, it is my great honor to introduce Gloria Newcombe."

Bang! went one of the Wedgwood dishes on the floor. Steve trembled all over. Albert, disturbed in his pleasant dreams, growled sulkily.

Then a familiar voice filled the trailer—almost as though she were back again, almost as though she had never gone away.

"Thank you, Randy," the voice said. (Gee, he'd forgotten how beautiful it was!) "I'm sorry my disappearance caused all this trouble. But perhaps you who are listening can understand that sometimes, no matter how dear are all the friends around you, and no matter how much you love your work, you just feel that you have to get away from it all and be alone. Far up in the north woods, I found the greatest happiness I have ever known. And until I can take time off once more and go back there, to rough it in the wilderness exactly as I did before, I sha'n't really be content. Perhaps the song I am going to sing will give you an idea of the simple life I mean. It was composed by a man for whose great talent I have the deepest respect and the highest hopes. I hope that he will write many more songs, for that is what he was born to do. If he is listening in, I hope he will like the way I sing it. He is a very critical composer."

Steve's ears, right next to the radio, began to get hot. There was silence for a moment, and then the orchestra played the opening bars of his own song. The voice that had moved him so deeply that day he had first heard it—singing the words he had scrawled down hastily one morning and almost forgotten—

> *"Trailing the sun,*
> *Trailing the moon:*
> *Hitting the highway*
> *Midnight and noon. . . ."*

Albert, suddenly wide awake, leaped off the bed and jumped at the radio. You couldn't fool him! He knew *that* voice!

Steve, swooning with happiness, reached down and grabbed him. Then he began to dance around the trailer, hugging Albert and laughing for joy.

XXI

THE tall and awesome admiral at the main entrance to the Waldorf blew his whistle imperiously and waved his hand.

"You can't park here, sir! Space reserved!"

Steve grinned at the admiral. "Sorry, old man. I thought you were saving it just for me. Look how nicely it fits." With a neat and expeditious twist, he edged the car—and the trailer—into the very center of the admiral's proud domain.

Flanked by two flunkeys, the admiral bore down sternly upon Steve. "Sorry, sir, but you'll really have to park somewhere else!"

Steve was out of the car and on the sidewalk. "But there isn't any place else. IIow much do you want for this lot? I'll buy it."

"Really, sir, the management—"

"Sold!" said Steve, pulling out a handful of bills. "Have a drink. Have sixty drinks. Loosen you up— teach you what you miss in life by always going around with a sour face. See you later—good-bye!"

And he dashed into the lobby and made for an elevator.

"Miss Newcombe's suite, please," he said.

"Miss Newcombe is seeing no one, this morning, sir."

"Good," said Steve, without batting an eye, even the elevator man's. "That suits me fine."

"I beg your pardon?"

"Come on, hurry up. Miss Newcombe will be impatient."

The elevator man sighed and shook his head. Famous people did the damndest things—and they had the damndest friends. Personally, he preferred business men. They were noisy, but they never startled you. Good, sound, steady noise—restful, by comparison.

He was glad to see this individual step out of his car and his jurisdiction. Snapping the doors shut, he sank back where he came from—to rise again, and sink again, and to go on rising and sinking, in the most intolerably dull and responsible way, for the better part of his life, no doubt. But that would be another story—all ups and downs, and hardly our affair.

As for Steve, his next trouble was the plain-clothes men who lurked in front of Gloria's door. He marched right up to them. "Good morning, Perkins," he said crisply. "I see that you are on the job. Thanks very much."

"Name ain't Poikins," said the larger of the two plain-clothesmen.

"Right!" said Steve. "I never forget a face, but names elude me. You're wanted at headquarters, Abercrombie."

"Oh, wise guy, huh? Listen, now—"

"Sorry, no time to give you an audition, Fitch. Good day to you." Steve dived for the door.

"Hey!"

'Nonny, nonny!" chirped Steve, stepping smartly inside and slamming the door in their faces. He felt extraordinarily gay, and capable of outwitting squads of admirals, generals, and even a couple of private soldiers for good measure.

Muffled thunder came from outside—he had locked the door after him. He looked eagerly round—it was very dim in here, hard to see—then he frowned as he saw a short, bulky shape rise and move toward him. More troops.

"Gloria!" he said, softly. Not a sound at first—then a muffled cry, a flurry of footsteps, and she was in his arms.

"My darling, my angel, my beautiful night-club queen!" said Steve. "My favorite star, my wonderful singer!"

Gloria was laughing and crying. "Steve, Steve, I thought I was never going to see you again—I thought you hated me."

The squat, bulky shade behind them sighed deeply. "*Excuse* me," it said.

"Certainly, Moe," said Gloria sweetly. "Be gone as long as you like."

*   *   *   *   *   *   *

"Listen, Abe, what'll we *do* with this bird?"

"*Do* with him? Listen, Moe, all the years I've been in pictures I have wondered why it is that you are allowed out of the booby house. Why did your mother unfortunately let you fall on the floor that time when you were a baby? Tch, tch."

"Listen to me, Abe, I have to take the bum jokes your comedians get off but it isn't in our agreement that I should take any from you. I asked you politely, what do we do with him?"

"Come sit down, my boy, and rest that brain of yours. I shouldn't want you to wear it out. Listen, you dope, if we can clear the tracks for this romance it will be worth millions! Millions, I am telling you! And he is asking what do we do with this gold-mine!"

"But how about—"

Abe lighted a long cigar, leaned back, and smiled. "How about that money-grabbing no-good who calls himself her husband, you ask? That's easy. His terms have always been easy to meet. Not bright, that fellow Jim. Nice boy, but he ought to've stayed in high school. I ship him to Mexico for a divorce by cable tomorrow—in ten days, Gloria is free."

Moe sighed again, and bit his fingernails. "Yeah, yeah, wonderful! And this musical genius fellow's *wife?*".

Abe fidgeted in his chair. "Don't ask too many questions! Let me concentrate. Millions, I told you! Shut up. Don't say a word. It's money she wants?"

"Money! When I had this Greene boy investigated I got the low-down from a fellow in his old man's office—name of McLeod, cold in his head. Damned if he didn't give me one too," groaned Moe, snuffling.

"Says the family has been trying to buy her off for months—and they're millionaires. So where does *your* million go? I ask you straight."

"Shhh, now! So she is a society dame?"

"One hundred per cent, horse, pants, big feet, the whole works."

"Perfect! Offer her a contract to appear in a super-colossal spectacle—tell her she'll be the star."

Moe looked at Abe. Abe looked back at Moe. A wave of profound understanding surged between them.

"Dummy concern?" whispered Moe.

"Shhh! Should somebody hear you?" whispered Abe.

*　　*　　*　　*　　*　　*　　*

Three days later, in the Ritz Bar, one tall bony girl with large feet said to another tall bony girl with ditto:

"My dear, have you *heard* the latest about Vivian?"

"My darling, *I* was the one who got it directly from her before she started for Reno. *Such* delirium!"

"Do you actually *believe* it?"

"Angel! She showed me her contract in black and white. She said the most amusing things about that ridiculous husband of hers! Admitted she never cared the slightest for him—as if everyone didn't see that from the very first moment!"

"I don't care, *I* thought he was cute!"

"Everyone saw that, too, dear."

"*Did* they, darling? Won't you have another olive in your Martini? *So* fattening! Oh, waiter! Another olive!"

*　　*　　*　　*　　*　　*　　*

A sheaf of telegrams in his hands, a bundle of letters under his arm, a smile upon his lips, and a gleam in his eye, Mr. Abraham Fancher stepped smartly into Gloria's suite that identical afternoon.

No longer was it a darkened suite; no longer did gloomy shades whisper in the corners; no longer did sour-faced bruisers with badges guard the doors. The sun streamed in through the windows; there were flowers everywhere; and Gloria, singing to herself, was standing at a window, gazing out over the island of Manhattan and approving of every bit of it.

"Where's the genius?" asked Abe. "I thought he'd be here. Don't tell me *he's* been kidnapped."

Gloria, smiling like a dewy spring morning, turned and walked towards him. "He's downstairs, seeing about things," she said.

"Seeing about what things?"

"Oh—just things," said Gloria.

"Well, anyway, I've got a new idea that's worth millions. Listen! Look at these wires. Look at these letters. Response from your broadcast. Response from that song. It's colossal! And it'll be better than that. The public is screaming for you in a new super-musical— singing his songs! Romance!" cried Abe, waving his hands and scattering telegrams all over the room. "Glamour! A perfect set-up! We'll sign him today. They'll go nuts. They're nuts already. Whew!"

"That's wonderful, dear!" said Gloria dreamily. "How lucky we are to get him!" ("Especially me," she said to herself.) "By the way, Abe, are there any fish in this picture?"

Abe jumped as though he had been shot. "Fish? Who said anything about fish? Listen, Gloria, can you forget the past for one little *second?* That's all I'm asking you. Since you came back it's all I hear from you—fish, fish, fish, fish! A man wants a change!"

There was a knock at the door; Gloria ran to open it. It was Steve—with his father and Moe, and a boy with a huge bouquet of flowers.

Gloria, usually so articulate, was wordless. She just stood and looked at Steve, and he looked back at her. Finally Mr. Greene, senior, spoke. "Well, I see you've got a lot to say to each other. As for me, I'm going to wish you luck and then I'm going to celebrate by taking a week off for some good fishing."

Gloria laughed; Abe smiled weakly; Steve whispered to his father and then to Gloria.

Mr. Greene beckoned to Gloria, and she followed him into the ante-room.

"I just want to have a little conference with my brand-new daughter," said Mr. Greene.

"Sure," said Steve.

"Sure, sure," said Abe and Moe. The dream of millions upon them, they beamed at everyone and everything. Gloria and Mr. Greene disappeared into the hall.

"Well, Steve," said Abe benignly, "I've drawn up the contract I spoke a little to you about. I've got it all ready for you."

"That's wonderful, Abe," said Steve. They were old friends by now—or rather, so far. Steve hadn't yet had a chance to see what working in pictures was like; so he grinned joyfully and signed his name.

Moe beamed at this happy scene. "You'll have true inspiration, Steve, composing for Gloria to sing—it's going to be wonderful."

"Wonderful?" cried Abe. "It's marvelous! We'll go to work right away."

"Well, not just this minute!" Steve said. "Because I—er—have to see a man about a dog."

"What? Oh, sure, we get it. Run along, take your time. Do a few hours make any difference?" Abe chuckled and smiled. Moe waved his hand gaily as Steve went out of the suite.

"Abe, didn't I always say there's nobody in pictures to compare with you?"

Abe grunted, and poured himself a glass of champagne. "Well?" he said, "and didn't I always agree with you?"

The two old friends and periodic enemies relaxed. Things would be fine now. No more trouble. No more complications. Smooth sailing, a calm sea, a rich cargo, everything perfect. Moe joined Abe over the champagne.

There was a soft tap at the door, and Everard Greene entered. "May I come in, gentlemen?"

"Sure, sure, glad to have you, Mr. Greene. Have some champagne. We'll celebrate."

Steve's father sat down and took the proffered glass. "Shall we drink a toast?" he said, smiling.

"We're *doing* it," said Abe.

"We'll do it *again*," said Moe.

"Gentlemen, to the happy runaways!" said Mr. Greene, and emptied his glass.

"Yes, to the happy—to the what?" cried Abe. He set down his glass and looked hard at Mr. Greene. Then he got up. "Where's Gloria? Where's Steve?" he shouted.

"Just a little trip, Mr. Fancher. After all, they're young. They've got plenty of time to work—later. Pictures can wait a bit, can't they? As a matter of fact, I'm going along. I need a week or two off. Mrs. Greene has promised to meet us—the proprieties, you know—"

"What!" Abe screeched. "Going fishing again? His face was an apoplectic hue. "I tell you they can't do it! They can't do that to me!"

Moe set down his glass, and clutched his head. Little Abe, without another word, ran for the door. Fairly leaping, he made for the elevator. Moe came panting after him. In a few seconds they were sinking downward —and so were their hearts.

Out in the lobby, they elbowed their way swiftly to the entrance, and confronted the admiral standing there, looking very mysterious and far-away.

"Listen!" gasped Abe. "I want just one piece of information. Did Miss Newcombe come out here a minute ago?"

The admiral looked mildly down at him. He nodded,

and tucked a hand absently into his pocket, as though there were something extremely valuable in it. "Yes, *sir!*" he said, and pointed up the avenue. Stricken, Abe and Moe gazed in the direction he indicated. Just pulling out into the traffic, and heading north, a familiar car, with trailer attached, appeared before their anguished eyes. There were a man and a girl in the car; and the girl, leaning out, was waving her hand.

At this moment, Mr. Greene, panting heavily, came running up. "Where are they?" he panted. "Where is the trailer?"

Abe and Moe were speechless—they could only point.

Mr. Greene looked—and slowly began to laugh. "So they've left me too!" he cried. "I thought when she kissed me for the third time this morning it was a sign of something."